ALIAS™

SHADOWED

LIZZIE SKURNICK

AN ORIGINAL PREQUEL NOVEL BASED ON THE
HIT TV SERIES CREATED BY J. J. ABRAMS

BANTAM BOOKS

NEW YORK ✸ TORONTO ✸ LONDON ✸ SYDNEY ✸ AUCKLAND

Alias: Shadowed

A Bantam Book / November 2004
Text and cover art copyright © 2004 by Touchstone Television

ISBN: 0-553-49440-6

Visit us on the Web! www.randomhouse.com

Published simultaneously in the United States and Canada

Bantam Books is an imprint of Random House Children's Books, a
division of Random House, Inc. BANTAM BOOKS and the rooster
colophon are registered trademarks of Random House, Inc.

PRINTED IN THE UNITED STATES OF AMERICA

OPM 10 9 8 7 6 5 4 3 2 1

Sydney awoke suddenly, having no idea how long she'd slept. In the dim light coming through the stamp-sized window in the door, she could just make out a figure standing at the foot of the bed. She jerked to a sitting position, her hands immediately coming forward in a defensive posture in front of her chest. In just two fast moves, either defensively or aggressively, she could disarm someone completely.

But it was Arvin Sloane—and he was empty-handed.

Sydney let her hands relax, but otherwise stayed tensed and upright on the bare cotton mattress. It was necessary, she sensed immediately, to stay ready for anything. She swung her feet around casually and placed them flat on the floor. Even in the dim light, she could see that one of Sloane's hands was on the doorknob, the other in his suit pocket, as usual.

If he was carrying a gun, Sydney decided, it was a very small one. *Anyway, if he were going to kill me,* she thought, *wouldn't he have done it already?*

You know, I used to hate when people assumed they knew all about me before they even met me. They'd see me in the undergrad library and chalk me up as a bookworm. Watch as I answered a difficult question in class and **whisper** that I was such a teacher's pet. Decide I was a prep because I had on madras shorts—or an athlete because I like to run often, and alone. Find out that as a kid I had nannies and went to boarding school and assume that I must be stuck up.

But now? Now I *like* when people think they know me. It's easy that way. It means I don't have to answer any questions. I can smile and nod and go with the flow while the world rushes past me.

They don't need to know that I'm flying **faster** than they'll ever go.

It's already October of my **sophomore** year. It's taken me twelve months, but I finally think I've got this college student/CIA agent thing under control.

Then again, I could be wrong.

"WATCH OUT!" A HOARSE voice hollered.

When she heard the shout, Sydney Bristow had only just swung open the steel door of the dim concrete corridor and stepped into the sunlight. There was no time to assess the threat, its danger, or the direction it was coming from—only time for her honed instincts to kick in lightning-fast. Before her conscious mind could even make a decision, her hand simply snapped out and plucked the disk from the air just before it plowed a dangerous path right into her face.

"Hey," her best friend, Francie Calfo, crowed

from behind her, quickly joining Sydney on the walkway in front of their dorm. It was fragrant with the rows of new blooms UCLA was always careful to plant at the beginning of every school year, when parents and donors were visiting. "*Awesome* catch!"

Grinning triumphantly at her roommate, Sydney flipped the Frisbee that had almost slammed into her neocortex over in her hands. Only two Greek letters decorated the back, but Sydney held the Frisbee up and squinted as if it contained loads of fascinating information. "Welcome back to UCLA, Sydney and Francie," she deadpanned, knowing that Francie, obsessed with her position in the campus popularity rankings, might fall for it.

Francie grabbed the errant Frisbee out of Sydney's hands. "It does *not* say that," she hooted, but her eyes flew open expectantly. When she saw that it was just another frat giveaway—the kind of logoed thingamabob that sororities and fraternities absolutely flooded the campus with during Rush Week—she gave Sydney a friendly shove and tossed the disk back.

"Coffee, roomie?" Francie asked.

Sydney looked around at the ragtag group of students scattered over the wide green lawn, throwing and drop-kicking a variety of plastic and rubber objects. It didn't look like anyone was going to come forward to claim the Frisbee—maybe, with the number of things whizzing around out there, its owner hadn't even noticed it was missing.

"Coffee," Sydney agreed, twisting around to stash the Frisbee in her half-open backpack.

Though she'd only arrived at the UCLA campus to officially kick off her sophomore year last month, Sydney felt like she'd never left. After a long night spent unpacking boxes, she and Francie had slept late—a rare luxury for Sydney—and spent the morning in the comfort of the fabulous new dorm suite they'd somehow snagged in the lottery. The dorm gods must have been looking out for them. The students who had originally won the suite had decided to study abroad at the last minute. The suite had opened up and—voila! They got it. And after an intense day of schlepping their stuff, they were in.

Nope, feels like I never left. And, as Francie keeps reminding me, I barely did, Sydney thought. *Ha! If only she knew.*

Though she'd now worked undercover as an agent for SD-6, a black-ops division of the CIA, for a year, Sydney still wasn't entirely used to the fact that reality and what she had to tell people sometimes had these pesky little differences.

As far as Francie knew, Sydney had spent her

summer exactly the way she spent her off-time during the school year: working at her supposedly boring job at a local bank, Credit Dauphine. And since Francie had capped off her summer with a two-week vacation visiting her parents, Sydney had thrown in her own vacation at the end, too: a relaxing week of camping on the Oregon coast.

Right, Sydney thought, thinking back to what she'd actually been doing those last few weeks—and, in fact, the entire summer. *Reeeeal relaxing.*

Because, far from a boring summer spent filing for a local bank, Sydney's past four months—the entire past year, in fact—had been one of the most difficult, exhilarating, confusing, and exciting of her life.

First, there was the little matter of the SD-6 training camp at Niagara Falls. In addition to brushing up on her spy skills in the competitive but supportive company of a group of new SD agents, she'd also been charged with retrieving a bunch of documents an eccentric scientist had hidden in the area. Instead, though, she'd somehow found herself *dangling* over the Falls themselves, battling for her own life and that of a fellow agent, against Paul Riley, a dangerous mole from the Russian crime ring K-Directorate.

Sydney wondered if it had been her success with that mission that had given Sloane, her handler at SD-6, the idea to send her directly into the heart of K-Directorate on the following mission. She still didn't know if the two missions were related—only that, undercover in K-Directorate, she'd finally met and battled Anna Espinosa, the organization's ruthless cover girl.

And I'm going to get her someday, too, Sydney thought, remembering with irritation how Anna had—but only just!—escaped her new agent grasp.

After that mission, Sydney had expected at least a few weeks off. But the release of some sensitive intel had necessitated that she jet off to Europe, where she'd gone undercover as the assistant to a dangerous magician. Discovering the secret to a series of mysterious paintings while learning the sophisticated arts of magic had been a complicated task, and at more than one point, Sydney had come close to disappearing herself—permanently.

Then, as if that hadn't been enough activity for the season, Sydney had been sent to Australia—this time as a rich equestrienne, with fellow agent (and quasi-boyfriend) Noah Hicks on board as her lowly servant. The stress of keeping up *that* charade through the mission—on top of the confusing, tumultuous, passionate feelings Noah had always evoked in Sydney—had nearly brought their still-young romance to the breaking point.

It's not that I don't love working for the CIA, Sydney thought, mulling over the enormity of what she'd accomplished in the few short months when most undergraduates were simply working minor day jobs or hanging out at the beach. *They just have no concept of downtime.*

"Well, at least it wasn't Alpha Kappa Chi," Francie was saying, dropping the name of the sorority she and Sydney had both rushed—then abruptly dropped—during their freshman year.

Sydney murmured her agreement before she realized she had no idea what Francie was talking about; she'd been daydreaming about her summer almost the entire way to the coffee shop. "Wait—at least *what* wasn't Alpha Kappa Chi?" Sydney asked.

Francie leaned over and plucked the Frisbee from where it stuck out of Sydney's bag. "This, doofus!" she said, gesturing to the Greek lettering emblazoned across the back. "I mean, then I might have worried it was actually personal!"

Sydney gave the lettering a closer look. Though it just so happened she'd recently brushed up on her Greek (for SD-6 agents, mastering five or six languages was the bare minimum), she would have recognized the letters sigma chi anywhere. Those same letters—each one five feet high—were pasted above the doors of a huge wedding cake of a house on frat row, a house particularly notorious for its rollicking, all-night blowouts.

Uch, Sydney thought, trying to block hazy memories of cigarette-choked ashtrays and burly football players spilling beer down the back of her shirt. *If I never go to another frat party again, it'll be too soon.*

But for Sydney, the memory of her and Francie's week in Hawaii with the Alpha Kappa Chi sorority was more than just an irritating memory of rich girls with way too much attitude and disposable income. Infiltrating the sorority had been one of Sydney's first SD-6 assignments—no way would she have joined on her own, thank you very much! And after Francie had found out that Sydney was rushing, Sydney had been forced to lie and invite her friend to rush the sorority with her, presenting it as a way for them to spend some much-needed time together. Francie, incredibly frustrated with all the time Sydney spent at Credit Dauphine, had been overjoyed. However, Sydney's mission—to find whoever had killed another sorority sister who was also an SD-6 agent—had spun out of control when she almost fingered the wrong sister—and since she had been busy tracking down a murderer, she and Francie hadn't actually gotten much of a chance to hang out.

Still, I hope Francie and I are in agreement about sororities, Sydney thought. *Four simple words: avoid at all costs.*

As if she'd read her roommate's thoughts, Francie shoved the Frisbee into her own tote along with the red sunglasses she'd been sporting and said, "I'm *so* glad we bagged on that one." She pushed open the door to the sunny coffee shop, which was filled to the brim with undergraduates, some with parents in tow. Then she turned to Sydney.

"Would it be an overstatement to tell you that I have more work to do in one week than I had my entire senior year of high school?" she asked Sydney.

"I bet that's an understatement," Sydney said, grinning. "But at least you're not chasing after sugar-amped kids anymore." In a spare moment, Sydney had spent some time with Francie and two of her young charges this summer, and she knew that despite her complaining, Francie really had taken to them. But she also remembered the hysterical e-mails Francie had sent her all summer about the various crimes that took place on her watch.

"*How* many times did their dog drag dirty diapers into the living room during your boss's dinner parties again?"

"Ohmigod!" Francie shouted, causing people at the neighboring tables to turn around. "Like, six hundred times!"

"You couldn't *pay* me to do that for a whole summer," Sydney said, suddenly thinking of the welcome checks SD-6 deposited into her bank account every two weeks. *Not that my CIA salary is really going to buy me a Jaguar any day soon,* she silently added, smiling.

"Okay, I'm officially sick of talking about school and work now," Francie said as they made their way to the back of the long line snaking up to three baristas, who were frenetically trying to make lattes and dish out biscotti as fast as they could. "We have two more important things to discuss: guys . . . and how we are going to decorate our new room!"

Sydney eyed the rows of delectable pastries and crisp, brown muffins underneath the counter. New room décor? Easy topic. Guys . . . not so much.

Though her year of working as an SD-6 junior agent had taught her to control both her body and her emotions in ways she'd never imagined she could, she still hadn't learned how to control the surge of guilt that accompanied every lie she ever had to tell.

The year before, the guilt created by all her lies—plus, though Sydney sometimes hated to admit it to herself, her *much* stronger feelings for Noah—had totally destroyed her relationship with Burke, an honest, funny guy Sydney had really liked and wanted to become close to. Over the summer, she'd made peace with the loss of Burke—and accepted the fact that working for SD-6 meant that lying to her best friend and those she loved the most was going to have to become a normal part of her double life from now on. Still, that didn't mean she had any intention of letting lies—the necessary, constant lies she had to tell to keep doing her work with SD-6—destroy her relationship with Francie.

"Do you want your usual?" Francie asked as she ordered *her* usual—a huge iced coffee—from the stressed-out barista who'd finally taken their order. Sydney nodded, glad to note that at least *one* fact about her—a notorious tea obsession—was completely and totally safe for her best friend to know.

Because there's already enough stuff it will never be safe to tell her, Sydney thought, watching as Francie laughed and chatted with the girl behind the counter.

But this year, Sydney had a plan. She was going to become more like her inscrutable handler, Sloane, whom Sydney could never read behind his smooth, deliberate smile. Or like her fellow agent, Noah, whose feelings *still* weren't always clear to Sydney . . . even when they were in the middle of kiss.

I need to develop a thicker skin, Sydney thought. *And I need to stop feeling like the lying I have to do for some job is so despicable. After all, it's for a good purpose—I'm working with the CIA!*

The rationalizing still wasn't working. The fact that Sydney couldn't tell her best friend the simple truth that her new, glowing tan was from the sun in Australia, not the Oregon coast, galled Sydney to the core.

Well, at least it was the same sun, Sydney thought as she and Francie looked for seats. *So why not be like Sloane is with his wife, Emily—concentrate on the stuff you* can *share, not the stuff you can't?*

"Ooo—a table. Grab it!" Francie said excitedly, pulling Sydney toward a group of hair-tossing cheerleader types abandoning a table near the door. "I've got all these plans I want to talk to you about!"

"Uh-oh," said Sydney, suddenly remembering a

prank Francie had insisted on playing on a snooty girl in their hallway last year. "The last time you had a plan, I seem to recall something about having to pay for twenty pizzas when the Domino's deliveryman star-69ed our number!"

Francie shook her head, smiling, as she pulled a sheaf of papers out of her tote bag. "Don't worry—I'm so over those childish games," she said. "Really, it's nothing like that—this is all about us and our amazing room."

Sydney smiled too, thinking of the huge, high-ceilinged new expanse they would call home this year. It was at least twice the size of their old digs—and the massive closets, hardwood floors, and four-foot windows opening onto a sunny green lawn didn't hurt either.

"Now, you know how the rust colors of the Southwest are totally like the ones in Morocco," Francie began, spreading what looked like at least twenty magazines' worth of glossy layouts over the tabletop.

"Like *The Arabian Nights*?" Sydney asked doubtfully, pulling one closer to peer at what looked, at least to her untrained eyes, like it must have cost thousands and thousands of dollars. She wasn't exactly sure how the cactus-and-Navajo décor of New Mexico that Francie had lived in for a few months had led to an obsession with punched-tin lamps, hand-knotted Persian rugs, and ancient-looking blue walls, but these layouts were an extremely expensive version of the type of rooms Sydney had actually witnessed on her missions in Morocco.

Well, she couldn't exactly mention that.

Still, I sure hope Francie's thinking of that, and not some awful Americanized version, Sydney thought, not sure how they'd be able to transform the admittedly large but still plain white room currently covered in what looked like thirty loads of laundry into one of the lavish layouts Francie was using for inspiration. A vision of her and Francie answering the door in identical flowing pink *I Dream of Jeannie* outfits rose before her eyes, and she had to stifle a giggle. Though Francie might get a kick out of playing that role, somehow she couldn't see herself melodically saying "Yes, master?" to anyone.

"So, isn't that *awesome*?" Francie asked. "Can you imagine the parties we could have?"

Sydney knew that once Francie's enthusiasm had been kindled, she was pretty hard to shut down. She opened her mouth to offer cautious agreement, but Francie interrupted. "You're going to love it!" she exclaimed, reaching across the table and squeezing Sydney's upper arm for emphasis as she fanned out some more spreads.

Sydney winced. That was the arm she'd injured when she'd fallen off the horse in Australia. Though her year of training had given her an astounding measure of control over her body's reflexes, it wasn't enough to block simple pain.

And she could tell that Francie had caught the almost imperceptible expression that flashed across her face.

"Syd, what is it?" Francie exclaimed.

"I . . . uh . . . pulled my shoulder lifting one of my boxes," Sydney hazarded, giving Francie a reassuring grin.

Luckily, Francie was easily convinced. "Dude, you need to take better care of yourself," she said, sucking up the last of her iced coffee. She gave Sydney a sly grin. "Especially . . . cuz I need help unloading all the supplies I already bought for Kasbah madness from Home Depot."

Sydney gave a loud groan. *If Sloane doesn't need me for a mission, Francie does*. She sighed inwardly. She could already see the next couple of weeks shaping up before her: slapping paint on the stark white walls, putting up a gazillion scarves and lamps Francie had enthusiastically purchased already, moving their furniture around for the millionth time. And that didn't even take into account the blowout party Francie would undoubtedly insist on having to christen their fabulous new surroundings.

Still, it's the least I can do, Sydney thought, bolting the last of her mint tea as she tried to remind herself how the preceding year had gone. *I mean, I was AWOL for a ton of best friend–type stuff last year. Besides, it might even be fun!*

"Ready, roomie?" Sydney asked, injecting as much heartiness into her voice as she could manage.

"Ready!" Francie responded, shoving the magazine pages back into her bag. As they exited the coffee shop, Sydney linked arms with her friend.

"We're going to have an awesome year in our new place," Francie said, bouncing on her toes excitedly.

"You know it," Sydney answered—for the first time, meaning what she said completely.

I'm just not even going to think about how I'm supposed to work SD-6 and my classes into it.

2

BY THE TIME SYDNEY and Francie had gathered up the last bags from Francie's car, it was nearly twilight. (Sydney hadn't been surprised to see that Francie actually *had* bought something like a thousand scarves.) Though most of the Frisbee addicts had cleared off the lawn—probably, Sydney thought, to head for the upgraded dining hall she'd been hearing about—there were a few stragglers tossing objects into the darkness.

"Um, so, do you think I bought enough?" Francie laughed as Sydney put down her bags to swipe her card key at the heavy door where she'd nearly been slammed that morning.

"Hey!" she heard from behind them. "Hey, wait!"

Sydney turned. Out of the darkness, one of the figures on the lawn was peeling off from his group and jogging toward them. As the boy approached, sweaty and out of breath, he pulled his baseball cap even lower on his forehead so that his face was completely hidden in shadow.

We should think about working this outfit into our undercover maneuvers, Sydney thought, checking out the guy's floppy shorts, sandals, and ripped, dirty T-shirt. *He's completely indistinguishable from practically every other guy on this campus.*

"Hey," Mr. Mystery said again, looking briefly from Francie to Sydney, then at the assortment of bags at their feet as he wheezed, trying to catch his breath. After a few more gulps, he finally spoke. "Um . . . I know this is a weird question," he said in a tentative voice. "But you wouldn't happen to have my Frisbee, would you?"

Immediately, Francie plopped down her bags, crossed her arms, and looked the guy up and down—not a good sign. *Uh-oh,* Sydney thought. She knew from experience that even though it wasn't that easy to get fun-loving Francie mad, once you did, it was watch out or be eaten alive.

"Do you mean the Frisbee you almost *killed* my friend with earlier?" Francie practically spat, her eyes narrowing.

The guy—whose face Sydney was still trying to get a better look at—threw his palms up. "Hey, I know!" he said. Sydney thought she caught the ghost of a nervous smile flit over his lips. "I was just coming over to apologize!"

But once Francie got mad, she didn't wind down easily. "Yeah, well, it's about time," she sputtered, her index finger rising for what Sydney knew might become a very ugly lecture. "You guys act like you're the only ones who exist in the whole—" she began in a threatening tone.

Sydney cut her off politely—if she knew Francie at all, she knew she had a long night of painting and hearing about the dreaded New Mexico toddlers ahead of her, and she wanted to get started on it. Also, she didn't want this fight—or almost-fight—to go any further than it already had.

"That's really nice," she said to the guy, hoping that would put an end to things right there. "It was no problem, really," she added as she leaned down to pick up the bags again.

But the guy had already intercepted her, offering his right hand for her to shake, like a salesman. "Brennan Daniels," he said, finally pushing back his cap. Sydney caught a glimpse of warm, friendly brown eyes and a wide, white smile.

But Francie was still on the warpath. "No problem!" she sputtered. "Did you know that you almost—"

"Sydney Bristow." Sydney cut her off again, sticking her own hand out and shaking the one offered her with a quick grab. "Listen, I've got your Frisbee in one of these bags if you need it back," she said, trying to move things along.

But Brennan had already moved on: to Francie. Extending his right hand confidently, he doffed his cap with his left, then placed the cap against his chest with a flourish.

"And this lovely lady . . . ?" Brennan asked, and moved slightly forward.

Ooo, that cheesy line's not gonna work on Francie, Sydney thought, sucking in her breath in nervous anticipation of the stream of invective she was sure would flow from Francie's mouth any second.

But suddenly the campus lights came on, illuminating the guy's warm brown eyes and dimpled grin. As if she'd been struck dumb, Francie stuck out her hand and shook Brennan's, and then flashed a slightly subdued version of her trademark grin.

"Francie Calfo," she said, her smile growing bigger as she took in Brennan's lean, tanned body and—even Sydney had to admit it—pretty cute smile.

That didn't mean she wanted to stand around chatting with the guy all night, though. *Great, now we're all BFs,* Sydney thought impatiently. *Can we go now?*

But for some reason, Brennan wasn't done yet.

"Um, I wasn't actually coming over just to apologize," Brennan began, flashing another nervous—and definitely cute—grin at both of them.

"Listen, I *told* you I've got your Frisbee if you want it back," Sydney said.

But luckily for Brennan, Francie was all ears. "Does it have anything to do with that fraternity on your Frisbee?" she asked, flashing a "let me handle this" look at Sydney.

"Um, yeah," Brennan answered, somehow looking relieved and even more flustered at the same time. "It's Sigma Chi. And we're actually having a party tomorrow night, so I thought you might . . ." His voice trailed off as he fumbled in his pockets for what Sydney knew would be one of the ubiquitous flyers frats always used to advertise their blowouts.

Ugh. Another stupid frat party? Sydney thought. *Thank God we're sophomores and know to skip it!*

"I don't know," Sydney began. "Registration starts Monday, and I was kind of hoping to get an early—"

But Francie had already reached out and plucked the flyer from Brennan's hand. "We'd love to," Francie said, hoisting her bags up again. "Now, if you'll excuse us, I've got to get my friend upstairs so she can get her beauty sleep."

"Awesome!" Brennan answered, smiling widely for the first time. Sydney hated herself for noticing his dimples . . . again. "Um . . . can I help you with those?"

Believe me, you've helped enough already, Sydney thought. "We're fine," she said.

Francie didn't even wait until they'd dumped the last of the bags on the shiny hardwood floor of their new dorm room. "Ohmigod. *What. A. Cutie,*" she said, emphasizing every word.

Sydney reached into the mini fridge, which she'd—thankfully—stocked with bottled water that very morning. "Who?" she said innocently, knowing it would drive Francie crazy if they couldn't gossip about their first genuine hottie interaction of the semester.

But Francie wasn't buying it. "He was *totally* checking you out," she said, reaching over for a sip of Sydney's water.

And, as if Francie's words had conjured something up, there was a knock at the door.

Sydney and Francie looked at each other and shrugged, Sydney getting increasingly irritated at her growing excitement. *It could be anyone,* she thought. *One of Francie's friends. The guys across the hall. Even another pizza deliveryman at the wrong door!*

But it didn't take SD-6 creds to figure out who it probably was.

With a sigh, Sydney pulled her now certifiably aching bones off the floor, ambled over to the door, and pulled it open.

There stood Brennan Daniels, holding a single, long-stemmed rose. Without a word, he placed it in Sydney's hands, bowed slightly, and turned to start back down the hall.

For a second, Sydney was too stunned to say anything. And once she found her voice, the question that came out of her mouth was anything but the subtle, incisive query of a master spy-in-training.

"How did you find our room?" Sydney called after him down the hall.

Brennan stopped walking. As he turned around, hands on his hips, Sydney saw that in the harsh light of the hallway, his slow, lazy grin was just as cute as it had been outside.

"Are you kidding?" Brennan asked. "The two most beautiful girls at UCLA?"

Sydney felt her face flush despite herself. Waiting until Brennan's footsteps faded into the stairwell, she slowly pulled the door closed, then turned to lean back against it, not ready yet to meet Francie's eyes. She looked down at the deep, flushed petals of the flower.

It was hopeless—she couldn't resist. She brought the flower up to her nose, buried her face in its petals, and sniffed deeply.

Sydney looked up. Francie, seated among a sea of plastic bags, paint cans, and assorted brushes and tarps, was slowly shaking her head.

"Well, well, well," Francie chuckled. "Looks like you've snagged the first cutie of sophomore year."

* * *

Francie had just pried open the first can of Royal Blue paint—her loose interpretation of the bright blue commonly found on the interior walls of Moroccan buildings—when Sydney's beeper went off.

"Sorry," Sydney said as she smiled at Francie, whipping her ever-present beeper out of the back pocket of the old cutoffs she'd donned for the room renovation. A quick glance at the beeper confirmed what she'd suspected: it was her handler, Sloane, calling her to a meeting at SD-6.

"Not the bank . . . ," Francie moaned.

Sydney shrugged, trying to look as unhappy as possible. Though it wouldn't make sense for her to be thrilled about being called into a dull day of filing at the bank she'd been working at since practically the beginning of freshman year, the truth was that each time her SD-6 beeper went off, it sent a little spark of excitement through her.

"Don't worry," Sydney said, quickly exchanging her cutoffs for the plain black skirt and white blouse that was a typical uniform at SD-6. "My boss probably just wants me to run through procedures with a new trainee or something."

Francie flopped back on her bed in frustration, her already paint-stained tennies churning aimlessly at the air like she was riding a bicycle. "How am I supposed to get this whole place painted without you?" she wailed, spreading her arms toward the walls of the dorm room, dotted here and there with her and Sydney's half-unpacked duffels and suitcases, like messy islands on a flat, hardwood sea. "I'll be lucky if I even get one wall painted before the party tonight!"

Sydney, dotting a little neutral gloss on her lips before slipping on her shoes and jacket, said nothing. She knew what was coming next.

Like a gymnast sticking a vault landing, Francie suddenly hit the floor. In the mirror, Sydney could look her directly in the eyes. "You *are* still coming to the party, right, Syd?" Francie asked.

Without saying a word, she walked to Francie and slung her arm around her roommate's shoulders, trying to transmit a feeling of regret in one big squeeze.

"Francie, I will *try,*" she said, trying to ignore her friend's furrowed brow, knowing full well she couldn't promise anything, no matter how much she wanted to.

After all, Sloane could just be checking in, or he could be sending me to Madrid tonight! Sydney thought, slightly ashamed at how her heart jumped at the thought that it could be the latter. *Well, wouldn't your average college sophomore pick an exciting journey over a crowded frat party?* she rationalized, trying not to beat herself up before she even got Francie calmed down.

"Honestly, if you miss this party, I'm totally asking Brennan out for coffee," Francie said, shaking her head sadly as she pointed to the flyer, which she'd thumbtacked to the wall near where Sydney had unceremoniously dumped the Frisbee and now-browning rose the night before. "Seriously—that's just too much cuteness to let go to waste."

Sydney was immensely relieved that—*this* time at least—it seemed that Francie could be distracted from Sydney's dereliction of her friendship duties by the thought of a mere boy.

"I will *try* to make the party," Sydney said, squeezing Francie's shoulder for emphasis and hoping against hope that her friend would forgive her. "But if I can't—you know what?" Sydney said in a sudden burst of inspiration. "I think he liked you better anyway."

3

"AGENT BRISTOW," SLOANE SAID with typical aplomb as Sydney threw open the glass door. She slipped into the nearest seat with as much composure as she could muster. "How nice of you to join us," Sloane added.

As usual, downtown L.A. traffic had been miserable. By the time Sydney had scampered through the Credit Dauphine lobby, descended into the parking garage that hid the infrastructure of SD-6, passed through the familiar body and retinal scan in its outer foyer, and done a flat-out run past the cubicles toward the conference room, she was a good twenty minutes late.

"Sorry," Sydney whispered to the ring of familiar faces already assembled at the table. In their usual seats, eerily lit by the blank video screen on one wall, were Sloane, Noah, and Graham Flinkman, SD-6's short—and often achingly long-winded—tech consultant. Also seated at the table were two women Sydney had never seen before. As she glanced at them, the one closer to her, a petite, spiky-haired blonde, gave Sydney a shy smile. The other—a brunette with large, slanted eyes and cheekbones that could have cut ice—didn't even bother to glance Sydney's way.

Let's hope that if I'm on a new team, I'm working with the blonde, Sydney thought nervously, wondering who the brunette was. *I thought working with Noah could be difficult, but this one looks like she could chew him up and spit him out like a piece of bubble gum.*

As if she could read Sydney's thoughts, the brunette suddenly met Sydney's eyes with a challenging glare. Sydney gave her a polite smile, an act that received only the faint lifting of one eyebrow in response.

"Sydney, I'd like you to meet Anya Mirofsky and Lucy Stell," Sloane said, smoothing his sparse beard with one hand as he lifted the other to gesture toward the tall brunette and the blond sprite in turn. "Ms. Stell will be working with Graham as our tech consultant for this project. And Agent Mirofsky"—he paused and smiled indulgently at the lanky, chestnut-haired beauty—"*Anya* was about to brief us on the situation when you came in, Sydney. In fact, I'll turn the floor over to her now."

Smooth move, Sydney—way to make a great first impression, Sydney thought, steeling herself at Sloane's words. She forced herself to take a deep breath, though what she really wanted to do was crawl under the table. Despite the tons of field and training experience she'd undergone over the past year, a meeting with senior agents could still make her feel like a . . . well, a dorky schoolgirl.

Across the table, the tech pixie—*Lucy Stell,* Sydney reminded herself, making a mental note of the name for later—smiled at her again.

At least I've got someone on my side, Sydney thought with relief.

Sydney couldn't believe what Lucy did next. After glancing briefly at Sloane, the slim blonde looked back and gave her a quick wink.

Sydney had no idea what to do. Was she supposed to wink back? Wave? Shoot her an irritated glance?

That's definitely what this Anya Mirofsky would do! Sydney thought.

But before she had a chance to do anything, she was immediately jerked back into the business of the meeting.

"Agent Bristow, I assume you're familiar with the case of Vitaly Radikovitch," Agent Mirofsky was saying, her voice menacingly soft. Silhouetted in front of the conference room's large screen— which now bore what looked like an aged passport image of a craggy-faced gentleman—Agent Mirofsky, clutching a pointer, looked for all the world like a dangerous raptor poised to strike.

Radikovitch . . . Radikovitch, Sydney thought, desperately hoping the name would ring a bell if she kept repeating it. *Who the hell is Vitaly Radikovitch?*

Making in impatient sound at Sydney's silence, Mirofsky pressed the pointer back toward the screen.

"As I'm sure the rest of you know," she continued, "Radikovitch was an extremely high-placed scientist for the Russian military pre-World War II, contributing many of the innovations that enabled their defeat of Hitler's troops."

"Sure, he was responsible for a lot of the developments in self-propelled artillery," Noah said as Graham and Lucy nodded. *God, am I the only idiot who never heard of this guy?* Sydney thought, glad the dimmed lights were hiding the flush of shame she felt rising to her cheeks.

"Radikovitch's top-secret workplace was in the Lake Baikal region of Russia," Mirofsky continued as a series of obviously weathered factory specs appeared on the screen. "When Hitler's troops moved through the area, they left the region decimated. These plans were all that has ever been recovered."

"Except for what Hitler's troops might have removed along the way," Noah cut in.

Agent Mirofsky turned to Noah with a wide smile. "Exactly, Agent Hicks," she said, in a smooth, intimate voice, as if she were telling a private joke. "Of course, historians have always assumed that the bulk of Radikovitch's work was lost. But with the fall of the Soviet Union and the Berlin Wall, documentation relating to numerous projects has flooded the black market."

Mirofsky tapped the screen and the image of the plans disappeared, replaced with the image of a handwritten letter. Though the script was tiny and the reproduction was not the best, Sydney could still see that the letter was written in Russian.

"Most of Radikovitch's work, of course, has been rendered redundant by the passage of time," Mirofsky continued, her English marked by only the faintest trace of an accent. "However, in this rare letter to his niece—which surfaced last year—we see a mention of what may have been the most top-secret project of all."

Mirofsky advanced to the next slide, which contained specs of what looked like some sort of small-scale firearm.

"Historians have speculated about the existence of plans for the so-called scalar pulse gun since the end of the war," Mirofsky said. "However, most assumed those plans were either lost—"

"Or had never existed," Noah cut in again.

Sydney, listening to Mirofsky's briefing, had almost recovered from her flash of insecurity moments before. But now, seeing Noah moving in lockstep with Mirofsky—practically *flirting,* Sydney thought wildly—she felt jealousy surge through her system.

In her months of studies and reports on the essential elements and implements of small-scale warfare, Sydney had heard, of course, of scalar pulse weaponry. Designed to be able to penetrate anything from the thinnest wall of a shelter to the thickest hull of a ship, it could penetrate pillboxes, fortifications, underground bunkers, and tanks and other armored vehicles, destroying all within. It was the holy grail of weaponry, the instrument that could render all other weapons completely useless, wiping people out without explosives, gas, or bullets.

The only problem was that no one—no one with any authority, anyway—believed that viable plans for a scalar pulse system really existed.

From what Sydney had learned, scalar pulse was now only the holy grail of conspiracy theorists and other assorted wackos. It was on the Cold War junk heap with other bizarre James Bond gear like jet-pack personal flying machines or Ferraris that turned easily into sleek motorboats.

And before Sydney could stop herself, her contempt was being voiced in the form of an irritated question. "Well, what is our proof that the plans *do* exist?" Sydney burst out, immediately regretting speaking aloud when all of the assembled faces turned to her in surprise.

"That's what we'll need you to find out, Sydney," Sloane said, indicating with one of his classic, decisive nods to Mirofsky that she could take her seat—which she did, though not before shooting Sydney a look of pure annoyance. "Recently intercepted intelligence suggests that these documents may in fact be part of a cache that Hitler never transferred at all—because he never had them," Sloane finished.

So did that mean they were heading to Lake Baikal itself?

"But Lake Baikal is enormous," Sydney pointed out. Geography had always been one of Sydney's strong points. Off the top of her head, she could remember reading that if you drained the huge freshwater lake, which was located near the Mongolian border, it would take all the Great Lakes of the United States to fill it again. "How could we possibly find a factory that's been gone for so long—especially when we never knew where it was in the first place?"

Sloane gave Sydney a patient smile. *Sydney, just listen!* she reprimanded herself inwardly. *How many times do you have to embarrass yourself— just keep your mouth shut and listen before you say anything!*

"As I was about to say, you won't be going to Lake Baikal. That is, at least," Sloane said, glancing quickly at Lucy and Noah and back to Sydney again, "not until you go to Berlin."

"But I don't understand—" Sydney began, and then actually had to physically restrain her hand from reaching up to her own mouth to smack it shut.

"If you had come in to the meeting on time,"

Sloane said, rising out of his normal calm to briefly raise his voice, "perhaps you would."

* * *

The rest of the meeting went down in a shame spiral, with Sydney listening in silence as the rest of the mission was relayed. It didn't help that Noah, as Sloane ticked off the final details, grinned intermittently across the table at Sydney as if everything she'd said that day had been for his personal amusement.

Noah, I don't get you, Sydney thought, watching his dark, hypnotic eyes across the table as he raised his pencil to add a comment or gloss on something Sloane had said. *The more I know you, the more I feel like I don't know anything about you at all.*

When they finally filed out of the meeting room, Sydney found that yet one more humiliation awaited her.

As Lucy, Sloane, and Graham headed off down the hall, Mirofsky pulled Sydney aside and looked deeply into her eyes. Up close, Sydney noticed, the agent was even more beautiful, with clear, smooth, glowing skin and bright green eyes—eyes that were narrowing as she looked Sydney over.

"Wool gabardine?" Agent Mirofsky asked.

For a moment Sydney couldn't believe her ears. Was it possible that the frosty arms expert wanted to talk . . . fashion?

"Um . . . I don't know," Sydney murmured in response, the thought briefly crossing her mind that this could be some kind of bizarre test. Had SD-6 instituted some new no-polyester clothing guidelines while she was down under?

"May I check your tag?" Mirofsky asked. She asked so calmly and reasonably that Sydney found herself turning around and lifting her hair out of the way automatically, as if swapping fashion tips in SD-6's bullpen was just normal post-meeting behavior.

Sydney felt Mirofsky's slim fingers glide briefly against the skin of her neck, then almost imperceptibly lift her jacket's tag out for inspection. "Hmmm . . . ," Mirofsky murmured.

Sydney couldn't help it—she was curious. As Mirofsky released the tag, she flipped her hair back into place and turned. "Gabardine?" Sydney asked, making a mental note to look up the term later. Maybe it was some new fabric Mirofsky had seen used on other agents in the field?

Mirofsky pursed her mouth and gave a tiny shake of the head.

"Polyester wool blend," she said, her slight accent and husky voice giving the words an improbable gravity.

Sydney felt the blood rushing to her face. *I can't believe a senior agent just busted me on my clothes,* she thought, trying not to let any emotion into her face. *Even worse—I can't believe how embarrassed I am about it!*

Mirofsky looked like she shared Sydney's embarrassment—only in a "Sorry you're so pitiful!" way.

"Well, see you tomorrow," Mirofsky said, giving her hair a tiny flip as she spun on her heel to head down the hall.

Sydney dreaded turning back toward the meeting room. There was only one thing that could make this situation worse, and she had a sneaking feeling that it had happened.

She swallowed and turned.

There, framed in the doorway, stood Noah Hicks, grinning absurdly.

"Aw, kid, don't worry," he finally broke out. "Synthetic fabrics have happened to the best of us."

To: Shadylady@mail.ru

From: Shadow@mail.ru

Re: Bugs and other crawly things

Pretty's tagged. Keeping watch.
Will advise further.

To: Shadow@mail.ru

From: Shadylady@mail.ru

Re: re: Bugs and other crawly
things

Excellent work. Until next.

"I DON'T BELIEVE IT!" Francie hollered, waving a blue paintbrush in Sydney's face. "Does your boss have any idea what *week* it is?"

Sydney still wasn't sure who was more freaked out—Francie, by the news that Sydney was being sent on a business trip at the beginning of the year, or Sydney, by the fact that their entire room was now a huge electric blue box.

Francie, covered with enough paint to look like a human Smurf, threw her paintbrush down on the drop cloth in frustration.

"Seriously, Syd, you need to learn to stand up to

your boss," she wailed. "You're a college student, not some high-paid executive they can keep on call 24/7!"

She'd decided to tell Francie the news in a good news/bad news way the minute she walked through the door of the dorm room. She'd been planning on throwing out the business trip first, then buttering up Francie with the fact that she was free for the party. Unfortunately, she'd been so shocked by the state of the room, and then overwhelmed by Francie's protests about her having to head back to work yet again, that she even hadn't had a chance to get the good news part in yet.

"Francie!" Sydney finally exclaimed, holding up her hand in what she'd learned through various missions abroad was actually the international symbol for *Please, shut up*. "You haven't heard the good news yet!"

Folding her arms, Francie took a seat beside Sydney on Sydney's bed (which was safely covered with a drop cloth and thus free of blue paint drippings, Sydney noticed with relief). "This better be good," Francie said, shaking her head.

Sydney felt her stomach turn over. She hoped once again that this year, SD-6 wouldn't drive a wedge between her and her friend.

Or at least that I can handle it if it does,

Sydney thought, realizing it was probably too much to expect that, with the way things were already going, SD-6 wouldn't come between them at all.

"I'm totally free for the party!" Sydney crowed.

For a moment, Sydney just waited. For almost a full minute, it didn't seem like Francie was going to react at all. But then, from what Sydney could detect through various eyebrow movements, fidgets, and sighs, it began to look as if Francie was trying to *look* mad, and failing. Finally, Francie sighed. "Well, I'm glad your boss has given you a *couple* of hours off, anyway," she said. Sydney felt a warm rush of relief surge through her system as a slow— but genuine—smile started to spread across Francie's face.

"Hey, I never showed you what I brought back from my nanny job, did I?" Francie asked.

Sydney shook her head, exhaling. If Francie was back to talking about her nanny job, that meant for *sure* that she wasn't going to yell. *Looks like I'm on Francie's good side—for now,* Sydney thought.

She began to run her hand idly over a heap of folded yellow, red, and pale green gold-threaded tapestries. Though each was delicately beautiful in its own way, Sydney was less than pleased to notice that each also seemed capable of clashing incredibly with the new blue walls. *I hope this trip doesn't take so long that this room totally runs off the rails,* she thought, wistfully recalling the simple but gorgeous white box it had been the day the girls arrived.

"Aha!" Francie said, yanking what looked like a tangled bunch of plastic webbing out of her suitcase, where she had been rummaging for the past five minutes. She looked slyly at Sydney. "Do you know what this is?" Francie asked.

A modern fruit basket? Sydney guessed. Then she thought of her recent mission in Australia. *A harness for a really tiny horse?*

"Um, I really couldn't say, Francie," Sydney asked. "I'm just hoping it's not wall art."

Francie came over and plopped the complicated-looking tangle of buckles and straps into Sydney's lap.

"It's the ChildSafe Leash System," Francie said, her eyes sparkling mischievously. "I used it on the kiddies whenever we went out in public all summer." Deftly, she fastened a strap around her own slender wrist, then secured Sydney's so quickly that Sydney had no time to even realize what Francie was doing—much less prevent her from doing it.

Um, that was kind of good, Sydney thought,

giving the strap a hard yank. It didn't yield in the slightest. *I have to remember that if SD-6 is ever looking for backup, Francie might make a good candidate.*

Francie stood up and began to walk toward the center of the room, dragging the thin rope of the apparatus behind her. The only thing missing from her cat-that-ate-the-canary smile was a stray feather on her mouth.

"It's forty feet long, so you can wander," Francie began, speaking to Sydney in the same "let's play nicely" voice that had been so completely ineffective on her unruly charges.

You know, this is one of those times it's really not fair for me to be a spy, Sydney thought, giving the apparatus a closer look. She figured it would take thirty seconds to crack, tops. Until that moment, she'd forgotten that one of her SD-6 instructors had given her the nickname Eel for all the complicated apparatuses she'd wiggled out of easily.

But I'm going to let Francie feel like she's winning for while, anyway, Sydney thought. Suddenly revealing Houdinilike skills to her roommate might count as one of those hard-to-explain situations a spy was supposed to avoid.

Still smiling widely at her friend, Sydney gave

the harness another subtle, but more strategically placed, yank.

She'd expected it to come apart in her hands. Instead, the smooth plastic remained utterly unaffected.

Hmmm . . . guess they're making these childproof things kinda hard-core nowadays, Sydney thought. Slipping her fingernail underneath the buckle, she tried to find the spring that she *knew* existed somewhere in the mechanism to release the lock.

Her fingernail met only smooth plastic. And there was still nothing.

Now Sydney was beginning to feel totally embarrassed. And there was another problem. Across the room, Francie was moving farther and farther back toward the far wall. Against her will, the extremely skilled junior agent was being drawn to a standing position.

This is ridiculous! Sydney thought. After all, she'd chased down terrorists in basement tunnels. She'd escaped from all manner of jails, holding cells, and physical restraints. She'd recently killed a spy who was threatening her friend's life, for Christ's sake.

Now she was being defeated by a piece of equipment designed to restrain two-year-olds.

Sydney dug her heels into the shiny hardwood floors and yanked back. It didn't do much good. Not only did Francie have the advantage, having the stronger position, but—as Sydney had, for some reason, forgotten—Francie, despite her love of glossy, perfectly manicured nails, kitten heels, and makeup in pastel shades, was also pretty strong.

Had Sydney not been mortified by how completely she'd been ensnared, she might have found Francie's look of smug, patient satisfaction almost . . . funny.

"Give it up," Francie cried, trying not to laugh.

"No way!" Sydney yelled back, wrapping another loop of the leash around her wrist. Her calves were already aching from resisting. She was damned if she was going to let Francie pull her completely across the room.

But that was exactly what was starting to happen.

As Francie backed farther and farther toward the wall, her glee finally turned to laughter. She suddenly released the leash, and Sydney found herself plunging headfirst onto the polished floor.

"Ohmigod, are you okay?" Francie called, rushing over. Splayed out in the middle of the room, Sydney was humiliated but unhurt. "I'm fine," she muttered. Making another fruitless pass at the wristlet, Sydney ignored Francie's outstretched arm and began to yank at the plastic ferociously with her full strength, banging her feet against the floor in frustration.

"What *is* this?" she finally gasped, flinging her hand toward Francie's still patiently extended hand. "It's like steel!"

Grabbing Sydney's wrist, Francie slid her finger underneath the offending strap, and in one smooth movement, the leash was off. Sydney rubbed at the skin, telling herself that she'd have to show the equipment to Graham sometime.

"Remember," Francie said, her face contorted with laughter as she held the leash up triumphantly. "This year, you're stuck with me!"

* * *

As they approached the Sigma Chi house on frat row, its windows and doors flung open, Sydney heaved a mental sigh of relief that, after a half-hour of discussion, she'd settled on jeans and a T-shirt instead of the minidress Francie had urged her to put on. The enormous and rowdy crowd spilling out onto the unmanicured front lawn of the huge Spanish-style house made her certain that this was definitely the kind of beer-spilling, Doritos-served-in-bowls party where it was better to be dressed for hard labor than fashion.

Back in the dorm room, Francie had shaken her head at Sydney's dull outfit and then admitted, "Well, I guess he's *already* psyched for you." As Francie watched, Sydney had calmly attached simple silver hoops to her lobes and pushed her brown hair—parted, as usual, in the center of her head—behind her ears. She wanted to fuss as little as possible, to keep from giving Francie the wrong impression. She tried to make it clear that she was attending the party as a friend to Brennan—and nothing more.

"Francie, please stop matchmaking," Sydney had begged. Once Francie got her mind set on something, it could be a little hard to steer her off of it. "Seriously, listen to me: this year, I'm completely swearing off men."

Last year's drama with Noah and Burke was enough to last me all through college, Sydney had added to herself. *If I've learned anything so far, it's that my life with SD-6 and dating definitely don't mix.*

Turning from the mirror, she'd checked out Francie, who was decked out in a flippy cotton miniskirt, an off-the-shoulder blouse, and long, dangly earrings.

"Well, if that means we can spend more time together, I guess I'm happy," Francie had replied. "But if you don't want Brennan, can I have him?"

Now that she and Francie had arrived at the actual party, Sydney only felt more strongly about the just-friends issue with Brennan. *He's definitely nice and all,* Sydney thought, looking with a slight feeling of butterflies at the usual-suspects crew of boys in baseball caps and girls with long, sun-kissed hair, all with beer cans and bottles of assorted shapes and sizes. *But I just can't see adding one whole person to my life to lie to at this point!*

Even one with dimples like that, she added silently.

As if he'd been able to hear her thoughts, Sydney saw Brennan—dressed now in chinos and a crisp white shirt, his dark curls looking adorably tousled—suddenly appear in the doorway of the Sigma Chi house. Slapping hands and smiling with the group gathered around the door, he began to make his way across the lawn, over to one of the crowded keg stands.

Before Sydney could stop her, Francie raised her hands, waved, and opened her mouth.

"Hey! Brennan! Over here!" she called.

"Way to play hard to get, Francie," Sydney muttered. She was annoyed to find that she was actually experiencing a flash of jealousy at how quickly Brennan—all dimples, grins, and tan, muscled arms—began to jog toward Francie like an eager puppy.

"Don't worry," Francie whispered to Sydney as Brennan came within hearing distance. He wasn't coming over alone: in his wake trailed two identically dressed frat brothers, also jogging toward the girls with eager grins on their faces. "I think I'm going to stick with his buddy there."

"Which one?" Sydney stage-whispered. There was a lanky redhead with a sprinkling of freckles, clutching a handful of what looked like—*Ugh!* Sydney thought—frat T-shirts, and another adorable shorter guy with glossy black hair and a muscled, smooth physique.

Francie barely had time to respond before the boys reached them. "Can't decide," she whispered, turning to Brennan with a wide grin.

"Guys! You came," Brennan exclaimed as he finally reached them. He grabbed Sydney's hand first, then gave Francie's a hearty shake. But as he gestured at his buddies, his gaze—to Sydney's slight embarrassment—remained firmly focused on her.

"Mark, Yun—meet Sydney and Francie, the

girls I was telling you about," Brennan said, slightly out of breath.

"Man, you did not lie," Yun said to Brennan as he gave Francie an even wider grin, only momentarily snapping his attention to Sydney. As far as Sydney could tell, the redhead, Mark—whose mouth was actually hanging a little bit open—was equally smitten with her glamorous roommate.

Hmmm, Sydney thought. *Guess she's not going to need me to pass Brennan off on her after all!*

"Can I offer you anything to drink?" Yun asked, finally gracing Sydney with a big smile and a firm handshake.

"Water," Sydney croaked out. Suddenly, she was incredibly thirsty. She was hoping she wouldn't look like a total dork for not drinking, but there was no way she was doing that tonight. She didn't mind a beer now and then, but, as she'd learned from experience, even the tiniest amount of alcohol the night before could cause a massive headache on the plane the day after.

And with Anya Mirofsky second-guessing her every move, she wanted to arrive in Berlin with all her wits about her, thank you very much.

"I'll go with you," Francie offered, giving one arm to Yun and then another to a slightly startled

Mark. She tossed her hair and gave Sydney a wink over her shoulder as the sudden trio walked toward the door. "See ya!" she said.

Really subtle, Francie, Sydney thought, silently cursing her friend.

But Brennan didn't seem at all perturbed—or, thankfully, even amused—by Francie's sudden departure. Lightly taking hold of Sydney's elbow, he gestured toward an iron bench that was set back slightly from the booming speakers and laughing crowds.

"Want to sit?" he asked, his eyes seeming to twinkle in the darkness. Taking a deep breath to offset the slight light-headedness she was feeling, Sydney told herself it was just the strobe lights the brothers had set up around the front for the impromptu grass dance floor.

"Sure," Sydney agreed. They moved over to the bench, neither looking directly at each other for a moment. The only sound was the roar of chatter and music coming from the party, now sounding almost impossibly distant in the night air, even though they'd barely traveled forty yards away.

Now that she and Brennan were alone, Sydney tried to steel herself to not make too big of a deal of the situation. *You're just sitting with a guy at a party, right?*

Brennan finally broke the silence. "So, Sydney," he said, leaning back to look her more fully in the face. He cleared his throat expectantly. "Why don't you tell me about yourself?"

Sydney laughed and looked back toward the partygoers. *Remember what you said: this year, no new guys.* Anyway, Brennan was asking a much more complicated question than he knew.

"Why don't you tell me about *yourself*?" Syd asked, using the no-fail policy she'd picked up to get herself immediately off the hook. She'd never met a college guy who wasn't totally happy just chatting on and on about how great he was and what was going on in his life.

But Brennan just raised an eyebrow, crossing his arms expectantly. Sydney sighed. *Figures. The minute I decide I'm not going to get involved with anyone, I meet the one guy who sends me clear signals that's he's totally into me,* she thought.

"Well, I'm from L.A.," Sydney began, trying to gloss over the parts of her life she'd never been thrilled to talk about since her mother's death. "I'm a sophomore. I'm thinking of majoring in history."

All of it true—especially the last part. After her humiliation at Agent Mirofsky's hands that afternoon, Sydney was feeling an especially strong need to brush up on her history.

Brennan uncrossed his arms and placed his hands on his knees. "It's great that you're so comfortable discussing your personal life," he said, poker-faced. "It's really rare, you know, to meet people who are so open right at the beginning."

Sydney laughed despite herself. "Well, what do you want to know?" she asked. "My shoe size?"

Brennan leaned in a little closer, shifting toward Sydney on the bench. "Well, how's this," he began. "My name's Brennan. I've got an older brother, David, and a younger sister, Mia. I like sea horses, coffee milk shakes, and salsa dancing. I'm not crazy about heights, but I love hiking. I also like swimming, but I'm not crazy about the sea. Go figure. When I got here I thought I'd be prelaw, but it turns out that econ is more my speed. I transferred from the University of Michigan after my freshman year because I couldn't take the cold. But you know what the real catch is?" He paused for effect, and Sydney shook her head. "I totally *love* to ski."

Brennan leaned back, a satisfied grin on his face. Sydney was impressed. And intrigued.

"Wow," she said. "I'm not sure I could rattle a list like that off if you gave me a few days to do it." *And even if I could, I'm not authorized to tell you most of it,* she added silently.

But now, Brennan made the move Sydney had

been afraid he'd make all evening. Across the teeny gap left between them on the bench, he reached for her hand.

She felt an electric jolt where he'd touched her, and, just like she'd touched a live wire, pulled away immediately.

"Listen, I really do have to get an early start tomorrow," she said, standing and trying to calm the sudden thudding in her chest. Still, she wasn't able to leave everything behind as if nothing had happened. "But if you want to get a cup of coffee in a few days, I'd love that," she added hesitantly.

Sydney was worried that Brennan was going to react with anger or get really uncomfortable, but either he was a really good actor or he was just as happy to pretend that nothing had happened.

"Totally!" he said, jumping to his feet along with her. "Let's definitely do it—soon."

After all, I said I wasn't going to get involved with any more guys, Sydney told herself as she walked back toward the party to see where Francie had gotten to. *But I didn't say I couldn't have any more guy friends!*

Sydney and Brennan quickly found Francie in the living room, seated on a dilapidated couch, happily chatting away with a circle of admirers.

"I'm going to head home," Sydney yelled over

the music, smiling apologetically at Yun, Mark, and three or four other guys wearing Sigma Chi T-shirts with their khakis. "Are you going to be able to get home okay?"

"I'll walk her home!" burst out Mark and Yun almost simultaneously. They glanced at each other sheepishly, then laughed.

"I think she'll be fine," Brennan said to Sydney in an aside, then, more loudly, added, "Sydney, I'll walk you home, if you don't mind."

"Oh, you don't have to," Sydney protested. If there was one thing she was sure of, it was that she could beat any campus aggressor in a fight.

Then again, there was no reason Brennan would know that. Also, though she was trying not to admit it, her heart was racing at the thought of making her way all the way back to her and Francie's dorm with only Brennan in the soft, warm night.

"I mean, you can if you want," Sydney finished lamely.

Without a word, Brennan leading, they began to make their way through the jammed, sweaty bodies out to the front door.

Watching his back, Sydney couldn't help thinking how, in a strange way, Brennan was almost a composite of Burke and Noah. All in one body,

Brennan somehow contained a kernel of Noah's smoldering, dark intensity, but with the gloss of Burke's friendly, easygoing openness on top.

Not coincidentally, those were the qualities that had drawn her to Noah and Burke in the first place.

Whoa, slow down, Sydney! she thought, trying to remind herself that things were already complicated enough with Noah as it was. *Remember—guy friend, not boyfriend!*

As they reached the end of the lawn, avoiding a gaggle of screaming girls, Brennan brushed up against Sydney's side. Shivers shot up from the backs of her knees to her cheekbones, and her side felt like it had been set on fire.

"This way or that way?" Brennan asked as they reached the end of the lawn.

Sydney knew he only wanted to know which route she wanted to take home, but she couldn't help hearing it as a question coming straight from her subconscious as well. Which way was she going to go? Was she going to let this go somewhere and risk putting another guy's feelings up against her job with SD-6 again? Or was she going to put a firm end to things now, knowing that concentrating on her schoolwork and her job with the CIA was the smart—if boring—way to make this year a *lot* less stressful than the one before?

Sydney stepped from the grass to the pavement, willing herself not to look back, to think of the mission ahead of her instead of the guy behind her.

"I can take it alone from here," Sydney said, already walking away. She could feel Brennan watching her as she stepped farther and farther into the darkness.

If he even bothered to say good-bye, she couldn't hear it. And there was only one thought going through her mind.

This no-guy thing is going to be hard.

OUTSIDE THE MUSEUM IN Berlin, in one of
SD-6's German command centers—actually a small,
nondescript van that appeared to be owned by a
small German air-conditioning systems company—
Sydney, Noah, and Lucy went over the plans for
what felt like the six hundredth time since they'd
flown over from L.A.

The basic elements of the mission were simple.
The Radikovitch papers had been recently uncovered
in a cache of World War II documents that had floated
out of private collections into public circulation after
the fall of the Berlin Wall. They were being kept in

the basement of the museum, in a climate-controlled environment attached to a lab where newer items were rigorously indexed and stored before being released into the public collection. That is, if they were deemed safe for release at all.

It was this area, Sydney noted as she once again examined the blueprints for the building, that she would be arriving at from above—winnowing her way down through the museum's air duct system from the room offered to qualified scholars to examine important documents. She'd find the basement off-limits to all but the museum's most qualified staff. According to the information Lucy had given Sydney and Noah during the technical portion of the briefing on the plane, the area wasn't watched by a human guard but by a sophisticated security system. That system was intricately connected to the cooling system that maintained the appropriate physical environment for the sensitive and delicate documents that were the museum's specialty.

Sydney's job was to scan the documents as quickly as she could, then get out. But for her to do that, the security system would have to be briefly shut off. Switching off the system to allow Sydney enough time to break in, scan the documents, and exit—and convincing the museum staff that there had only been a normal and temporary shutdown of their system for repairs and upgrades—was Noah's job.

Lucy, still as spiky and cheerful as ever, would be handling the tech portion of the goings-on. As Sydney had learned from Noah on the flight over, SD-6 was grooming her to be Graham's assistant and wanted to check out her skills in European technology.

Setting the wig she'd be using for the mission firmly in place, Sydney once again gave a silent thank-you to Sloane for not assigning Agent Mirofsky to the mission. *As if this wig weren't itching me enough already,* Sydney thought. *She'd probably make fun of me in this outfit for hours!*

Her hair pulled under a long, strawberry blond wig, Sydney wore the horn-rimmed glasses, tweed suit, and subdued makeup of the Ph.D. candidate she supposedly was. From the glances she'd had in the mirror, she already knew it wasn't her most flattering look. Still, she knew that there was no way Noah was going to start ragging on her. His rugged good looks were partially obscured by a workman's cap. He also wore the white jumpsuit of the museum's security company and carried the computerized report pad and toolbox the company representatives used on their visits to perform security updates.

Lucy, looking even smaller than usual with her

massive headset and three refrigerators' worth of equipment surrounding her, seemed as confident, laid-back, and comfortable to Sydney as she had that first day in the conference room.

"Let me check your ears," she said to Sydney. Sydney leaned over and pulled back the wig to let Lucy run a last-minute scan on the almost invisible earplug that allowed the entire team to communicate during the procedure.

Sydney and Noah's mikes were new technology, replacing a slightly bulkier system from the year before that had been prone to feedback and distortion. Sydney's was hidden neatly in one side of her glasses. On the flight over, Lucy had demonstrated how, if Sydney chewed the stem in a thoughtful manner, her mouth would be positioned for maximally clear transmission—though actually any position would work in a pinch. Noah's mike, easily enough, was planted directly into the fake company walkie-talkie he carried as part of his equipment. As he worked to disconnect the security system, any statements would simply be taken as normal chatter with the home office.

In an especially smooth move, the camera Sydney would use, designed by Graham and Lucy together, was the right-hand lens of her glasses. To photograph a document, all she had to do was hold it up in her field of vision and run her hand lightly over a small button on the right-hand arm of the frame. To the outside observer—or to anyone watching the security-camera feed—she would only appear to be adjusting her hair as she peered more closely at some fascinating item.

No doubt about it, Sydney thought. *The gadgets we get to use are totally the best part of this job.*

"Milton," Noah began, addressing Sydney with the code name she'd been given for the mission. "You'll approach the information desk at—"

"Fourteen hundred hours," Sydney finished, pulling a few stray strands of hair from under her jacket collar, where they were itching her. *Note to wardrobe: ditch the synthetic wigs.* "And after I'm safely inside the scholars' room, wait for your call," she added, not missing a beat.

"Noah," Lucy said, giving Sydney a wink and waving her off. "Let me see you for a second."

When they'd boarded the military plane for Germany eighteen hours before, Sydney had been especially glad to learn that Mirofsky, instead of accompanying them, would be supervising the mission from SD-6 headquarters. Unfortunately, the entire flight over—that is, the part before they all crashed into the deep sleep field agents usually trained themselves to be able to drop into at a moment's notice—Noah insisted on talking about nothing but Agent Mirofsky.

"So she's got a master's in fine arts from the Sorbonne," Noah said, tapping a pencil against what Sydney recognized as his most weathered, most broken-in pair of jeans. "But get this: she also did a Ph.D. on global trade at the London School of Economics."

Sydney wasn't sure if the nausea she was feeling was the roiling result of all the turbulence they were suddenly experiencing or the reaction to Noah's sudden interest in the leggy new agent.

"That's great," Sydney said, wondering whether Noah would get the hint if she pulled out her notes for the mission and began to examine them yet again. Unfortunately, the last three times she'd tried to indicate that she was less than open to the conversation, Noah had regaled her with the information that Anya had emigrated from what was then the Soviet Union to America when she was nine, that she'd been orphaned at sixteen when her mother, her only living parent, had died of lung cancer, and that, based on her stellar academic performance and scores on various standardized tests, she had been admitted to Harvard University.

Maybe it was time to try a new tack. "How did

you find all this out?" Sydney asked over the hum of the jet engine. She didn't allow herself to ask the obvious question, but she thought it: *And are you trying to tell me something?*

Noah grinned. "Sneaked a peek at her file," he said.

Sydney was appalled. Though she'd met Sloane's wife, Emily, and Graham chatted about his personal life all the time, there was nonetheless a code of secrecy around the office toward colleagues' private lives. Higher-ups knew all there was to know, sure—but fellow agents were always on a strictly need-to-know basis about personal details.

Does this mean Noah knows everything about me, too? Sydney thought. *Like . . . how bad I am in history?*

"Dude, I'm *kidding*," Noah finally broke in— filling Sydney with relief. (She was no tattletale, but that didn't mean she was on board with the idea of Noah taking some cockeyed tour through all of SD-6's personnel files.) "Anya and I had a chance for a cup of coffee before the meeting, and she filled me in on some of her background."

Does that mean you also filled her in on our *background?* Sydney thought, noticing how Noah's eyes kept lighting up every time he imparted some new tidbit. Their relationship was of necessity a major secret at SD-6. Still, watching Noah discuss Agent Mirofsky with obvious admiration, Sydney couldn't help feeling that she wouldn't have minded Noah giving Mirofsky a little hint about whose turf was whose.

"Noah, why are you telling me all this?" Sydney finally broke in.

From Noah's shocked face, it was clear that she'd succeeded in getting through to him that she'd prefer that he knock off his lecture series on the personal life of Anya Mirofsky.

"Jeez, Sydney," Noah said, shaking his head. "If you haven't figured out yet that this business runs almost exclusively on intelligence, then I can't help you."

Listening to Lucy's light snores, they spent the rest of the plane ride in silence.

* * *

The van pulled into a dark alley to drop Sydney off. As the plan directed, she'd arrive on foot and enter through the front, where, as Ilsa Tannenhaus, she had an appointment with the museum's archival director. Then Noah and Lucy would pull the van around back, where Noah would use the service entrance and meet up with the museum's director of operations.

I hope Noah's not getting a complex, Sydney thought, closing the van's door behind her, scanning the alley to make sure no one had seen her descend. *Maybe it's the fact that he keeps playing handyman that's making him irritable!*

But despite their almost-fight in the plane, Sydney wasn't worried about working with Noah. If she'd learned anything from their many missions together, it was that whatever was happening with them personally, when they were working together, they were all business, focused completely on mission.

But as she propped open the door of the van and held out a small mirror to determine that no one was watching from any angle, Sydney couldn't help admitting that there was a pair of twinkling brown eyes, a bright smile, and a low, witty voice in the back of her thoughts at all times, distracting her from what was happening in Berlin and sending her squarely back to California.

She could not get Brennan Daniels out of her head.

Shaking it off, Sydney flipped out of the van, moved onto the street, and melded with the other businesspeople walking to and fro on the busy Berlin sidewalk. She tried to concentrate on keeping her pace smooth and even, but an idea was tickling the back of her mind.

If Noah's moving on to Anya, maybe it's time for me to move on too.

Sydney reached the sleek granite steps that led to the museum's door. Checking the area around the museum briefly—and noting the ancient security guard who sat in a drowsy stupor just inside the museum's glass doors—she willed herself to focus on what she had to do in the next five minutes, not the next school year.

Syd, right now, concentrate on getting the documents for SD-6, she told herself. *You have the rest of your life to worry about Brennan Daniels.*

It was a strange and new feeling to be so distracted by thoughts of an *outsider* on a mission, Sydney thought as she moved confidently up the steps. Of course, ever since she'd started working with SD-6, she'd experienced strong feelings for Noah as they completed their various missions—she was only human, she reminded herself. But Noah was right there in front of her face—it was natural for her to be thinking about him. As her partner and senior advisor, he was woven into the fabric of her work as tightly as the bright threads embroidering fanciful patterns on Francie's Moroccan scarves.

Brennan had nowhere near that kind of shared

history with her—and she'd barely just met him. So
why couldn't she get him out of her mind?

Sydney entered the museum, which she knew
had once been the grand residence of a wealthy
banker. To the right of the airy but small marble
foyer sat a receptionist at a shining walnut desk. Behind her, an open doorway led to a hallway of
decidedly more modern offices. The holdings of
the museum, Sydney reminded herself, were mainly
contained in its two modernized basement levels,
while public collections and private scholar's rooms
were found in the three upper stories.

The museum was almost like a rabbit warren,
Sydney observed, calmly approaching the desk.
*Which means there's lots of ways out—but lots of
wrong turns I can make, too.*

"Guten Tag," Sydney said to the receptionist in
her calm, impeccable German. After the receptionist murmured a polite response, Sydney, hoisting
her briefcase to her other hand, continued, *"Ilsa
Tannenhaus für Herr Janklow?"*

Within minutes, a tall, dapper gentleman wearing a sleek gray suit and rimless glasses emerged
from the back offices. He approached Sydney with
a look of polite anticipation.

A museum that specializes in maintaining the

*integrity of paper documents and personal corre-
spondence probably doesn't get a huge number of
visitors,* Sydney thought, taking care to compose
her face in a professional mask.

"Fraulein Tannenhaus?" he asked, extending
his hand.

Sydney held her hand out, hoping her slightly
dowdy clothes and lank hair jibed with the look of the
small assortment of scholars who usually made use of
the museum's curious collection. "Pleased to meet
you," she told the director in German, uttering a silent
prayer that several German study modules in the past
year had rendered her accent completely indistinguishable from that of the current young Berliner.

"I was quite intrigued with the paper you submitted," Herr Janklow commented, leading Sydney
past the receptionist's desk through a side door
she'd glimpsed as she'd walked in. " 'The German
Housewife and the Rise of Fascism'!" Herr Janklow stopped completely, turned, and gave Sydney
a delighted smile. "Really, quite fascinating!"

Okay, let's cut the chatting, Herr Janklow, Sydney
thought, surreptitiously glancing at her wristwatch
as he turned back and continued. Noah would be at
the service entrance by now, and Sydney had to be in
place in the reading room when he began "upgrading"
the museum's security system.

"Well, I felt it was an important subject," Sydney said noncommittally, trying to add a frosty tinge to her voice to discourage further conversation. Though Sydney had, of course, scanned the paper SD-6 had submitted to the museum on Ilsa Tannenhaus's behalf, she hadn't had anything to do with its creation. That honor went entirely to SD-6's crack team of analysts, who had formulated their bogus research based on the hottest trends in academia. Though Sydney personally couldn't see what housecleaning had to do with Hitler, even she had to admit that, as she'd skimmed it, the paper *had* been quite convincing.

"I'm very flattered, of course," Sydney added after a moment. Somehow, the jacket around Herr Janklow's shoulders had seemed to sag momentarily, as if his feelings had been hurt.

The SD-6 team had set up Sydney's appointment around one of the museum's largest collections: thousands of letters that had been exchanged by German housewives during the various wars in the country's history. The collection had been gathered in the 1960s, but it included series of letters from as far back as the 1860s, all the way up to the period following World War II.

Sydney knew that scholars examining collections usually did so in a series of visits—sometimes stretching over a couple of years if they were writing a book or a huge thesis. However, Ilsa Tannenhaus would only visit once. Imagining the paperwork SD-6 would send out on her behalf, Sydney thought it was likely that Ilsa was about to lose the grant money that allowed her to continue her graduate studies in the first place.

At one time some of the incredibly complicated maneuvers SD-6 went through just to get information had often seemed wildly over-the-top to Sydney. When she'd first begun her training, pumped up to use some of the kicks, jabs, and physical moves she'd been learning—to say nothing of the fancy equipment she'd been introduced to—Sydney had wondered why SD-6 didn't just go in and take by flattery or by force (as safely as possible, of course) exactly what they wanted. After all, they were the CIA, backed by the U.S. government. Wouldn't other countries naturally want to cooperate—or be scared not to?

But besides the fact that that would have focused way more attention on SD-6 than could ever be allowed for it to safely operate, Sydney had learned that leaving any trace of SD-6 involvement conflicted with one of Arvin Sloane's dearly held principles. There was nothing, absolutely nothing

Arvin Sloane liked better than obtaining some tightly guarded piece of information—except, of course, obtaining said information without anyone having any idea how—or even *that*—he'd done so.

"Fraulein Tannenhaus," Herr Janklow said. They'd reached the end of the hallway and gone up a flight of stairs, and now the director was gesturing Sydney into a large room with windows on three sides. Filled with shelves and shelves of neatly filed beige portfolios behind glass doors, the room was easily recognizable to Sydney from the blueprints of the building she'd examined earlier. It was the reading room, the place where she would be allowed to examine files she had already requested and that the museum had pulled on her behalf.

And if all went well, she'd be examining some other files too—some the museum had not given her access to.

"If you'll take your seat here, Frau Schmidt will bring the first series of documents," said Herr Janklow. With a slight bow, he led her to a seat in a row of wide, heavily polished oak tables lined with dim, green-shaded lamps. "I trust you will have a productive session."

Sydney settled herself into one of the deep, surprisingly heavy chairs and opened her briefcase, trying to look businesslike and efficient. "Thank you very much," she said, pulling out a sheaf of papers and a pen.

Herr Janklow had taken one or two steps towards the door, but when he gave a brief glance back toward Sydney to smile politely, what he saw made him freeze him like a statue.

"Oh!" he exclaimed in alarm. Like a jackrabbit, he sprang back to the side of Sydney's study table, a look of absolute horror on his face. Sydney had just enough time to hide her transmitter under a sheaf of fake notepapers before Janklow reached her. The small device allowed Sydney, Noah and Lucy to experience distortion-free communications during the mission.

His breath coming in short, angry pants, Herr Janklow did not hesitate. Firmly and a bit angrily, he leaned down, reached over, and plucked the pen from Sydney's hands. With a flourish, he placed it decisively in his right coat pocket and stood up ramrod straight.

"Absolutely no pens or writing implements of any kind in the reading room!" Herr Janklow said, his previously measured tones gaining in volume and acquiring a slight edge of hysteria. "As you were informed in the documents we sent you ex-plaining our scholar's practices!"

Sydney tried to keep herself from panicking,

though she could feel a blush spreading from her neck to her cheeks. Master spy or not, it was just really unpleasant to be yelled at like a disruptive child.

Okay, keep it cool, Sydney reminded herself. *There's only one thing that's really important here. Whatever you do, you've got to keep Herr Janklow from examining the contents of the briefcase.*

"Of course, Herr Janklow!" Sydney said, forcing a wide and polite smile across the stiffness of her cheeks through sheer will. The gears in her brain started working overtime to find the credible lie that would make Herr Janklow depart with as little difficulty as possible. Instead, he opened his mouth and lifted a finger, looking like he was about to give the dreaded lecture and search request Sydney desperately needed to avoid.

"I was *just* going to hand that to you," Sydney quickly cut in, adding a slightly irritated tinge to her own voice, trying to sound as if she were just as annoyed as Herr Janklow at the breach of the museum's protocol. "I believe our departmental assistant must have put it among my papers in error," she finished. Giving what she hoped would pass for an embarrassed laugh, Sydney held both her hands out in a "What can you do?" gesture, then shook her head as if this were just one in a line of equally annoying incidents.

Herr Janklow, breathing heavily, gave a slight nod and seemed slightly mollified. Taking a crisp white handkerchief from his pocket, he swiped it across the sweat beads that had popped out across his forehead.

"You understand, of course, that we must be extremely careful with the collection," Herr Janklow breathed. Returning the handkerchief to his pocket, he gestured toward a row of shiny new computers across the back wall.

"You may, of course, use the computers to take any notes you wish," he continued. "We can also provide copies of any selections to you within three weeks." Herr Janklow straightened his tie and seemed to collect himself. "For a fee, of course," he added.

Yes, Herr Janklow, I will *be needing some copies,* Sydney thought. *But I'll be making them myself, thanks.*

Sydney knew that it was imperative that she get rid of Herr Janklow as quickly as possible. Noah would be contacting any minute, giving her the go-ahead to break into the room one story below. And in the meantime, she had to photograph the pertinent documents here in the reading room. The last thing she needed was an anal busybody hovering over her while she attempted to get away with unauthorized intelligence.

Luckily, Sydney knew exactly how to get rid of him.

If there's anything I've learned being a spy, Sydney thought, thinking back with amusement on how often she'd used the technique during the past year, *it's that the only way to get rid of a busybody is to pretend to be even busier.*

"Herr Janklow, many thanks," Sydney said smoothly. "Now, if you'll excuse me, I'm eager to get started with my work."

And, like a puppet on strings, Herr Janklow snapped to attention. It was clear to Sydney the director of the museum's archives respected an assiduous and aggressive display of industry.

"Of course, *fraulein*!" Herr Janklow said, giving another bow. From his apologetic expression, he'd seemingly forgotten about the pen incident completely. "I'll see what's holding up Frau Schmidt."

As Herr Janklow exited the room, Sydney allowed herself a small exhalation of relief. She adjusted her glasses, trying to keep calm, knowing that even though Lucy had checked them at least four times, technical snafus still happened. Could that be what was keeping Noah?

Moments later, an attractive middle-aged woman entered the room. Not even bothering to acknowledge

Sydney, the woman put down a large portfolio in front of Sydney, turned on her sensible, scuffed heels, and left.

Even though the woman's shoes were clunky and dowdy, Sydney noticed, she had been dressed in a fitted gray suit whose fabric moved easily over her body, lending her a tidy, professional look. Ever since Anya had commented on the quality of her suit fabric, Sydney had been noticing a lot more about people's clothing in general.

But there was no time to think about that now. Ever mindful of the state-of-the-art security cameras mounted against the antique crown molding of each of the room's four corners, Sydney removed the black band from the portfolio's heavy cardboard covers and began removing the first of several dry, brittle documents. If Herr Janklow was taking a little peek to make sure his scholar wasn't whipping more pens out—or, God forbid, writing with them—Sydney wanted to make sure everything looked normal.

And then, just like that, Noah's voice came, clear and strong, over the earpiece of Sydney's glasses.

"Milton, I'm going to need you to get in position," Sydney heard. She could just picture Noah hunched over a tangle of wires and a computer screen, getting ready to make the slight adjustment that would give her approximately thirty seconds to take a series of photographs of the documents they needed.

Casually, Sydney moved her glasses to her mouth and gave a studious chew. "Got it," Sydney said. "I'll alert you when I'm in position."

Placing her glasses firmly back on her nose, Sydney stood quickly and headed for the door. Out on the landing, she nearly crashed into Frau Schmidt, who was carrying a box filled with more folders. Thankfully, Sydney managed to grab it before the contents toppled to the floor.

"Oh! *Mein Gott!*" Frau Schmidt exclaimed, taking the box back with a grateful nod. "Is there a problem?"

Sydney pointed toward the door on the landing that she knew contained a ladies' room. Frau Schmidt nodded sagely and disappeared behind another door off the landing. "I'll be back with your next round of papers in just a moment," she called over her shoulder.

Damn, Sydney thought. Knowing that Frau Schmidt was constantly tripping back and forth through this section of the museum added another layer of stress to the task she had to complete. Now she'd have to be even faster—and quieter—than they'd planned. After all, Noah's clock was already running.

Stepping across into the small powder room, Sydney quickly locked the door behind her. She'd have only a few minutes out of the view of cameras—a few minutes to shimmy down through a series of ducts, take the photos, and work her way back to the bathroom, then return to the reading room without anyone knowing that anything had occurred.

Hopefully, it would go as smoothly as the mission had so far.

"Donne, I'm above the target," Sydney said, not even bothering to remove the glasses. "Are you prepared for the interruption?"

Noah's voice, as always on missions, was completely void of emotion—if he was feeling one ounce of the stress surging through Sydney's veins, she couldn't hear it.

"Milton, ready here," Noah replied. "Please advise when you're at target."

"Copy that," Sydney said. "Central?"

"Ready here," Lucy chimed in.

It was time. Quickly, Sydney stripped off the blouse, skirt, and too-large boots she was wearing, twisting the wig's strands into a tight knot at the back of her neck. Underneath, she wore a stretchy catsuit and ballet flats with hard-gripping soles that were much better suited to what she was about to do. The only item that remained from Sydney's original outfit were the glasses, which she plunged into the v-neck of the catsuit, where a padded pocket waited. Every time Sydney had tested this portion of the outfit, she couldn't help feeling like some hokey Old West madam twisting a roll of bills, then placing them safely in her cleavage— even though Graham and Lucy had emphasized that it was the easiest way to ensure the mic's functionality during this part of the maneuver.

Leaning down below the sink on the hard tile floor, Sydney ripped off the sleek neoprene sheath she'd had strapped around her upper arm the entire mission. In the sheath she'd find a screwdriver, clamps, mini crowbars, and other brushed-steel tools that could handle almost any situation an old building could offer.

Or at least, Sydney hoped they could.

Under the sink was the vent Sydney was aiming for. After a moment of difficulty, she easily removed the screws, and then pulled off the grill. A dusty square faced her.

It was dark inside that square. And—despite SD-6's preparations—a pretty tight fit.

Good thing I've been jogging a lot lately, Sydney thought as she restrapped the slim tool belt to her arm, pulling on a pair of thin gloves that gripped just like the soles of her shoes.

She wasn't looking forward to the next portion of the journey.

Agents usually used a small forehead light—like a mini version of a miner's—when they had to shimmy through the ducts of a building. However, the path Sydney had to take was so quick and direct, she'd eschewed the full-out regalia.

She was regretting that choice now.

Taking a deep breath, Sydney plunged in, making her first movements hesitantly. The extremely close-walled shaft she was traveling through had been part of the building since its construction, a heating duct for an ancient furnace that had long since been retired. There was just no telling what type of nastiness was in there now.

But Sydney didn't have time to dwell on the horrors in her imagination: scurrying rats or dust so thick it could have doubled as peat moss. She leaned fully into the shaft, pulling herself along toward the square of light that would allow her to drop down to the basement level. As she worked her way along, inch by irritating inch, she lay on her side, her shoulders against the top of the shaft, her hipbones against the floor.

Luckily, there were no huge dust wads—or rats—to be seen.

Hey, maybe that paper was right, Sydney thought, inching around a corner that forced her to twist like a gymnast to squeeze by. *Germans are way better housekeepers than anyone else.*

Flat on her belly, she looked in front of her, where she was supposed to see the square of light that indicated the grill on the ceiling of the documents room.

There was nothing.

No! Sydney thought. *They've closed it off!*

But it had only been a trick of her eyes, unused to the darkness of the small enclosure. When she blinked again and leaned slightly forward, she could see it: the thin line of the grill that would lead her into the main archiving room.

Sydney couldn't help it—she felt a surge of joy, as she always did when the target was ahead. She tried to quell it—there was no reason to get happy until she was safe on the plane, with the pictures already transmitted to SD-6.

Until then, it was bad luck to feel anything.

Inching her way forward, Sydney worked her hand up to her upper arm for the tool strap. She'd have only seconds to undo the screws on this grill—then she'd simply have to wrench the entire thing up and pray for the best. Hopefully, she wouldn't bend the frame so much that it would no longer rest in place when she was done, but she'd have to worry about that when and if it happened.

The crowbar was in her hands. But first, she had to get Noah to turn off those pesky cameras.

"I'm in place," Sydney murmured into the mic. "Please copy."

"Copy that," Lucy replied immediately. "Donne, are you in place for shutdown?"

"Copy that," Noah replied. Even though Sydney knew he was probably sweating out this part of the mission, she couldn't help thinking how he sounded for all the world as if he were lying out near a pool on a beautiful sunny day, taking his first sip of a frosty lemonade as he flipped open a magazine.

"Initiate in three," Lucy said calmly. A sudden whirring sound on her or Noah's end carried over the wire to Sydney. "That's three . . . ," she continued, "two . . . and one."

Even in the shaft, Sydney could hear it. It was like standing on a white street after the first big snow of winter—instead of hearing the loud noise of life, you suddenly noticed only its total absence. The whirring of the climate-control system of the museum—and its attendant security system—was gone.

Sydney had to act, and fast.

Shimmying as quickly as she could, she pulled herself over to the grill. Four quick moves yanked the rusty metal screws out, still in their holes. Quickly placing the grill aside, Sydney braced herself against the sides of the hole and then dropped to the floor below.

There was no alarm. Noah and Lucy's shutoff of the system had worked.

Surrounded by rows and rows of flat gray metal filing cabinets, Sydney found herself in the center of a strikingly clean basement room. There was no light from street-level windows except for one tiny casement window opening in the far corner. The corner cameras regarded Sydney, blank and still. Now it was time to get to work. She only had a few minutes before Noah would be forced to put the system back up.

According to SD-6 sources, the Radikovitch papers were filed under his name. Taking in the labels on the front of the long file drawers, Sydney rushed across the room and yanked one open. If all went well, she'd be able to photograph every piece in the file and then get out of there without any trouble.

Except that she was hearing the unmistakable sound of footsteps on the stairs.

Panicked, Sydney looked around for a place to

hide. Behind one of the filing cabinets? It was impossible. There was only an inch between the back of each and the plaster wall. There was a flat gray metal table, but anyone would be able to see a person crouching beneath it.

And the footsteps were getting closer. She had to make a decision.

In three swift moves, Sydney raced across the floor back toward what seemed to her like the gaping hole in the ceiling. Hoisting herself onto the top of a filing cabinet, she swung herself upward, the tips of her fingers just grazing the ragged edges. Plaster crumbled and came away in her hand.

Someone began to push the door open, and the overhead lights, with a flickering hum, came on.

Bracing herself against the ledge, Sydney pulled herself back into the shaft, hoping against hope that whoever was entering hadn't caught sight of her feet vanishing into the ceiling.

But there was no time to think. Gripping the grill with the tips of her fingers, Sydney placed it tightly and gently back into its hole.

"So you see," Sydney heard a female voice say in a perfunctory, dry tone, "here is where you will be working with Professor Schlegel."

"Ah, yes," said a much younger voice. It could

have belonged to a high-voiced boy or a deep-voiced girl.

Sydney sighed with relief. Clearly they hadn't heard anything. And it appeared that someone was only showing a prospective intern or a low-level employee around.

But the young voice was coming closer. "May I examine this piece of equipment for a brief moment?" it asked in a wheedling tone.

If this student or whatever hangs around, there's no way I'm going to be able to complete this mission! Sydney thought, dry-mouthed. *Not a chance!*

As if Noah had somehow been able to overhear, his voice suddenly came up in Sydney's earpiece.

"Status, Milton?" he asked.

There was no way Sydney could respond. Even if she kept her voice at an almost inhumanly low level, the room was dead silent. They might not be able to hear her, but they'd hear something.

And Sydney's hiding place would be blown.

But whoever was showing the young person around suddenly took control. "Absolutely not, Friedrich," she said in a crisply efficient voice. "It is forbidden to even touch the equipment without a team member's supervision."

Sydney slowly exhaled. *Figures,* she thought. *A place that doesn't even let its visitors take a pencil in with them isn't going to be big on people "examining" the equipment.*

And her time was still running out.

But the sound of the first set of footsteps started receding. Then the overhead lights snapped off, and the door swung slowly shut. Sydney heard both sets of footsteps traveling up the stairs again.

"We had some visitors," Sydney said slowly into the mic. "But we're back on track now."

* * *

The rest of the mission went swimmingly. Before she knew it, Sydney had completed the photographs of the entire Radikovitch file and was up the shaft again. She replaced the grill in the small powder room, redressed in her Ilsa costume, and unlocked the door.

Frau Schmidt was standing outside of it, holding another large portfolio.

"Did you find everything you needed?" Frau Schmidt asked politely. "I thought there might be a problem."

Sydney forced herself not to look behind her. She *knew* that the bathroom was pristine, she *knew* she'd replaced the grill, and she *knew* she'd left nothing behind. She'd given it a thorough 360—twice—before exiting.

It was sometimes hard not to get nervous and second-guess herself, though.

Sydney assumed what she hoped was a suitably haughty expression.

"Everything is fine," she said, moving swiftly past Frau Schmidt into the hall. "May I?" she asked, holding her hand out for the folder.

*   *   *

On the plane ride home, Noah and Lucy were jubilant. All in all, the system had only been down three minutes. Noah had left without incident; the museum's security director was convinced that their system had only received one in a series of periodic upgrades. And Lucy was thrilled that her method for disabling the system remotely had worked so swiftly and completely, allowing her to get it back online the minute Sydney confirmed that she was back in the reading room and the pics had been transmitted, through the glories of satellites, directly to SD-6.

"You did a great job," Noah told her, squeezing her arm. Sydney smiled back happily. Noah's praise was rare, and she'd learned to savor it whenever she got a rare taste of kudos Hicks style.

"Thanks," she said, before dropping off into a deep and dreamless sleep.

Later, as they were preparing to deplane, Lucy tried to make plans with Noah and Sydney for a "celebratory martini," but Sydney was anxious to get back to Francie and see what sort of disaster the room was in currently.

"Sorry—I've gotta get some more rest," Sydney said. Besides, even though she liked Lucy, she'd much rather it be just she and Noah.

Noah flashed Sydney a look, but she couldn't read it at all. Had he wanted to go out with Sydney also? To speak to her about something? Like . . . Anya?

But Sydney didn't have time to think any more about what was going on between her and Noah. As the door of the jet was thrown open and a rush of warm L.A. air blew in, instead of the usual bare tarmac, she saw a black sedan parked at the bottom of the staircase. Two big men in flapping suits, hands folded, stood next to it.

"What the . . . ?" Noah asked. Lucy's face wrinkled in confusion.

As Sydney reached the bottom of the staircase, one of the men walked forward.

"Sydney Bristow," he said. It wasn't a question.

Sydney was too shocked to say anything. The other man approached, blocking off her exit path.

"Hey, what's going on?" Noah asked more aggressively, fumbling his way toward Sydney's side. One of the men held up his extremely large hand.

"Agent Hicks, please stand down," he said. "This doesn't concern you."

Before Sydney could object, the other beefy man took her by the arm, slapping a pair of cuffs on her wrist. He began to lead her—not gently—toward the waiting vehicle, while the other man restrained Noah from interceding.

Sydney couldn't believe what was happening. She took as firm a stance as she could against the pull of the larger man—which was reminding her eerily of her battle with Francie and the Child*Safe leash a few days earlier.

"Stop this! What is going *on*?" Sydney screamed.

The window of the car began to descend. "That's what we'd like to know," came a voice from inside the car, easily audible to Sydney, Noah, and Lucy, who'd been watching it all from a few feet back. And, as Sydney watched in horror, the speaker stepped out.

It was Arvin Sloane.

6

IT HAD ONLY BEEN twenty-four hours, but Sydney felt like she'd spent a lifetime in the small, bare cell.

Sydney's arrest and detention by SD-6 had happened so quickly that even almost a full day later, she'd still barely been able to process the events so that they made any sense to her. One minute, equipment slung around her shoulder, she'd been heading off the plane from Berlin onto the tarmac, the warm evening breeze, very welcome after the stuffy plane's cabin, blowing through her hair and cotton clothes. The next minute, she'd been handcuffed, blindfolded, and stuffed none too politely into the back of a roomy and totally untraceable government vehicle.

Bracketed on both sides by the meaty arms of two SD-6 goons she'd never seen before in her life, Sydney had known better than to try to make an escape or try to glean any useful information from the muscle-bound guards. Still, as the silence in the car grew, and as fear settled into the pit of Sydney's stomach like a heavy ball of wet cement, she couldn't resist asking one question.

As it turned out, it was the wrong one.

"Where are you taking me?" Sydney asked.

Sydney was using all her mental strength to keep her voice from shaking. She could feel the car's speed picking up, and scenarios were rushing through her mind as quickly as the slight bursts of light she could still see under her blindfold from the streetlights they were whizzing by. Was she going to be deported for some crime she didn't know she'd committed? Was she being taken directly to federal prison? Or to some other, infinitely more horrible place where the CIA brought agents that had . . . displeased them?

Another thought buzzed through Sydney's

mind, quickly turning the ball of cement in her gut into a bomb on the verge of detonating. *Has SD-6 taken Noah into custody too?*

The goons shifted at Sydney's question, squeezing her like a vise at the mere sound of her voice. As her small rib cage was compressed still further, Sydney began to regret that she'd said anything at all.

"You'll see," one of the goons finally allowed. To Sydney's relief, he also shifted slightly away, allowing her to relieve some pent-up anxiety in a whoosh of air and fill her lungs completely and comfortably for the first time in a minute or two.

Now, looking around the bare cell, Sydney still couldn't tell where she was. She knew the car ride had been relatively quick (though to Sydney it felt like it had lasted years). With such a short ride, it was possible that she was being kept in SD-6 headquarters, in some sector of the building to which she'd never been given access. She knew the building had more than enough room.

Though she was obviously on the outs with Sloane, the fact that she was possibly being held at her good old place of work gave Sydney an odd measure of comfort. *That bumping I hear at night—it could be Noah walking right overhead,* she thought.

But of course, as Sydney well knew, SD-6 had

installations all over the world—and all over L.A. *I could be one floor down from the SD-6 boardroom,* Sydney thought, *or under a cactus in the middle of the desert.*

There were certainly no clues from her surroundings. The cell where she was being kept was a box about six feet square, bare and hard. It was set up to defeat the canniest spy or escapist, as Sydney had discovered in her frantic examination during her first hour inside.

Of course, SD-6 isn't going to teach me how to get out of a jail cell, then build cells that its agents could escape from in their sleep, Sydney thought unhappily, rubbing her now free wrists.

The room was windowless, of course, with a cot bolted to the floor, a seatless, stainless-steel toilet and sink, and a polished concrete floor. Other than the bed frame and the toilet—both forged out of a single piece of metal so they couldn't be pulled apart—the room was empty. Sydney's only views into the outside world were the small, Plexiglas square on the industrial door to the cell, with its metal sliding tray for her to receive her meals, and a tiny bread-loaf-sized vent through which clean air was circulated into the room.

There was no chance of shimmying through this vent like she had at the museum in Berlin, though: it was located directly in the center of the ceiling, about fourteen feet over Sydney's head. And even if she could reach the vent by vaulting up somehow from the bed, it was way too small for her to fit through—that is, unless SD-6 was thinking of starving her for a few months into confessing.

But confessing what? Sydney thought for the millionth time. The question, which had been repeating in her brain with all the regularity of the Chinese water torture ever since her detention, had stopped evoking terror in Sydney ages ago. Now, as the hours ticked on, and as the cell became smaller and smaller and the questions bigger and bigger, not knowing the answer only brought a dreadful feeling of loneliness.

It was the kind of utter, harsh loneliness Sydney hadn't experienced since her mother's death when she was a child. Then, she'd been careful not to show any hint of the fear she was feeling to her father— thinking for some reason that he might be mad at her, that she might even be responsible somehow. But at night, in her bed, she'd wept alone, knowing that there was no one she could go to.

And the question she'd asked herself was the same.

What did I do? Sydney thought. *What could I have possibly done to cause something like this?*

Hours and hours before, after going over all the events of the past couple of days, Sydney had decided that her detention couldn't be related to anything as simple as a basic mission failure. First of all, there'd been plenty of goof-ups in her work—alongside, of course, a number of successes.

So maybe I messed up somewhere along the line, Sydney thought, going over conversations and maneuvers for what felt like the zillionth time. *But Sloane must know—at least I hope he knows—that I'm a valuable member of the SD-6 team.*

After all, wasn't that exactly what people had been telling her?

Sydney leaned back on the bare bed with a groan, one of the first exterior signs of distress she'd allowed herself during her imprisonment. She was making sure not to show too many emotions—or movements—of *any* kind. Though she hadn't been able to find the barest hint of one anywhere, it was likely—almost *certain,* in fact—that there was a camera somewhere, transmitting its feed of Sydney Bristow directly into the office of Arvin Sloane.

Which could actually mean that this was not entirely the tragedy Sydney thought it was. It could mean that this was something Sydney had never expected but that she better damn well acquit herself in.

An SD-6 test.

It wasn't as crazy an idea as it seemed, Sydney thought, going over the possibilities again in her mind. After all, it was the anniversary of her first year as an agent—exactly the time you might expect your kindly employers to bump up the stress and make sure you really *were* ready to play with the big boys. Also, Sydney thought, Lucy's and Anya's sudden appearances on the SD-6 team argued that everything might not exactly be business as usual.

After all, though SD-6 staff did come and go, it wasn't exactly Grand Central Station in the boardroom. Not only would that open up the facility to penetration from outside agents, Sydney reminded herself, it would be antithetical to SD-6's Mafialike credo: in for one day, in for life.

Except mine, Sydney thought. *Because for whatever reason, I've been cast out of the SD-6 safety net.*

And it better not be for good.

Sydney thought again of the sudden introduction of Anya and Lucy. Lucy, on the one hand, made total sense—Graham had been angling vocally for an assistant to groom for as long as Sydney could remember. But Anya, on the other hand, was a real wild card. Was she an agent in another SD branch? She hadn't been introduced as such. And why was she such an expert on the Radikovitch situation?

Why weren't SD-6's own analysts able to provide the type of intelligence and direction Mirofsky had provided? Heck, Noah had seemed up-to-date on most of the intel she'd provided in her briefing, anyway.

Sydney's head was spinning. She laid it down on the bare, pillowless pallet that passed for a mattress.

Another thought suddenly occurred to Sydney: that Mirofsky's rudeness could have been part of a test too.

Please—that's really stretching *it,* Sydney thought, her overselling of the concept already depleting the faint emotional lift she'd briefly felt at the possibility that her imprisonment was some well-orchestrated sham. *Somehow, I don't think standing up to mean girls is high on Sloane's list of what he needs from his agents.*

Also, putting aside the fact that she couldn't exactly see Sloane toying with agents when he could be sending them off on perfectly useful missions, Sydney had to admit one irritating truth: the feelings in her stomach she always depended on to let her know what was up in the middle of a dangerous situation were telling her that what she was going through was all too real.

And that truth, rather than destroying Sydney's will, was helping her keep it together. If this was *real life,* she kept reminding herself, she was going to have to bring all her skills to bear to get through it. She didn't have time to weep or go crazy. She didn't have one iota of energy to waste.

Not even on stressing out, Sydney thought.

There was, of course, one more obvious answer to what was keeping Sydney in the cell. It was another reason she was keeping cool and alert and trying not to let anything shake her. Because if this wasn't a test and it wasn't just some horrible mistake, there was only one explanation for Sydney's imprisonment.

She was being set up.

So far, all signs pointed to that option. Of course, they also pointed, from Sydney's perspective, to a black void. Because until she'd figured out why she was being held in the custody of SD-6, she couldn't figure out who was trying to set her up, or why.

She wasn't going to make a move until she knew at least one of those two things. It would only get her deeper in hot water—or worse, killed.

Right after the goons had removed her from the car and transported her, still blindfolded, to the cell, there'd been a moment when she'd considered escaping—or at least making a desperate effort to escape. She hadn't been sure she would succeed—

in fact, she'd have been lucky if she'd found herself evenly matched against even one of the hefty guards. Still, she'd defeated outsized opponents before. She'd also escaped from some pretty tight situations—it was what SD-6's experts had trained her for, after all. But the moment had been lost, and now Sydney desperately wished she'd taken the chance, no matter how steep the odds had been. Because now, listening to the hum of the vent as she surveyed her dull, industrial surroundings, Sydney was increasingly coming to believe that some horrible person was planning something very, very bad on her behalf.

Curiosity killed the cat, Sydney thought, resting her boots briefly on the bed frame's edge, and then rising to go into a series of basic stretches for the twentieth time since her imprisonment.

But satisfaction brought the cat back.

7

SYDNEY AWOKE SUDDENLY, HAVING no idea how long she'd slept. In the dim light coming through the stamp-sized window in the door, she could just make out a figure standing at the foot of the bed. She jerked to a sitting position, her hands immediately coming forward in a defensive posture in front of her chest. In just two fast moves, either defensively or aggressively, she could disarm someone completely.

But it was Arvin Sloane—and he was empty-handed.

Sydney let her hands relax but otherwise stayed tensed and upright on the bare cotton pallet. It was necessary, she sensed immediately, to stay ready for anything. She swung her feet around casually and placed them flat on the floor. Even in the dim light, she could see that one of Sloane's hands was on the doorknob, the other in his suit pocket, as usual.

If he was carrying a gun, Sydney decided, it was a very small one. *Anyway, if he were going to kill me,* Sydney thought, *wouldn't he have done it already?*

"Sydney," Sloane said, his voice almost ludicrously casual and uninflected, considering their current circumstances. "Feel like a talk?" he asked, lifting his chin slightly.

Sydney hadn't brushed her teeth or washed her face since the Berlin mission. She felt filthy, tired, and, most of all, terrified. But those years as a little girl dealing with her grief alone had had their effect. She was *able* to deal with being alone and scared, able to function when everything she trusted had been suddenly ripped away.

So there was no way Sydney was going to let Sloane see even a trace of what she was feeling. Not until she knew what was going on—and whether there was a magnum of champagne or a firing squad behind the door. Not until she knew whether the man she'd served for the past year was her protector or her executioner.

Whether this is a test or not, Sydney thought, rising to her feet as steadily as she could, *keeping calm and blank is going to be the only way I'm going to get through it without going completely bonkers.*

Sloane inclined his head slightly to the left and then held the door open for her. Sydney didn't speak. She'd already decided she wasn't going to answer any of Sloane's questions until he'd answered some of her own.

Like—first of all—where in the hell am I, Sydney thought.

Sydney brushed past Sloane, experiencing a slight moment of embarrassment as they came within a few inches of each other. She knew she probably smelled awful. Embarrassment was overcome by fear, though—fear that only grew as she moved through the door and found herself in a bare, empty corridor lit by a row of flickering fluorescent bulbs.

Well, I'm definitely not going to figure out where they're keeping me from any clues in this hallway, Sydney thought, turning around to face Sloane. *And this certainly doesn't seem like a good time to ask.*

Sydney had expected to find the two goons outside the cell, and there they were, hands clasped in front of them.

I wonder if Graham designed these guys from some goon model? Sydney thought with irritation. *Did he also program them to look like they enjoy strangling puppies in their spare time?*

Sydney still wasn't sure yet how angry she was with Sloane—that would have to wait until her boss revealed what was going on—but almost having her rib cage crushed by the deep-voiced duo in the back of the car the other day had earned *them* her enmity forever.

Without uttering another word, Sloane turned from Sydney and began to walk down the hall toward the steel utility door at the end. Flanked by the guards, Sydney had no choice but to follow. Each step she took echoed slightly in the rounded, submarine-like hall, followed by the goons' heavy steps. Sydney couldn't help thinking that their procession seemed horribly close to the walks inmates took on Death Row in the movies.

She just hoped that they weren't walking toward her personal electric chair.

Thankfully, as Sydney and the guards passed through the door at the end of the corridor, what she saw around her wasn't anything close to a death chamber. Instead, she found herself in another narrow corridor, this one much closer to a typical office setting, with beige carpets, cubicles, and windowed conference rooms. Unfortunately, unlike a real office—or like SD-6's ultramodern, buzzing setting—this place was completely empty.

Well, so much for the "Surprise!" and streamers theory, Sydney thought. *Definitely no party here.*

Still, she began to relax, though only slightly. *This is no place to kill or torture anyone,* Sydney thought. *It looks more like the kind of place you'd take someone to conduct a job interview—or an audit.*

Was this what they did to agents who didn't pay their taxes?

Sloane walked past the first row of cubicles and then stopped in front of a large, nondescript door. One of the guards opened it and pushed Sydney in. Her heart sank. The room, practically empty, contained only a table with one chair on either side. The left wall was mirrored.

A standard interrogation room.

If this is a test, they're really working it to the hilt, Sydney thought. *Where'd they get those guys, anyway—the WWF?*

Sloane, a small, polite smile gracing his features, gestured wordlessly for Sydney to take the seat farther from the door. As she walked around the table, she watched in the reflection of the mirror as one of the goons pulled the door shut from the hallway.

Presumably, they would be waiting outside .

Sloane took the seat closer to the door, letting the smile spread across his features. Sydney couldn't help feeling relieved by the fact that it was Sloane she would be speaking to. Even though he was her boss, she'd gone to his house for dinner and met his lovely wife, Emily. He wasn't going to do anything bad to her. Right?

His hands clasped on the table in front of him, Sloane finally broke the silence.

"Well, Sydney, here we are," he said.

Um . . . that's the understatement of the year, Sydney thought. The obvious statement didn't deserve a response, and she didn't give one.

Sloane looked into her eyes. "Do you have anything you'd like to tell me?"

Though it had never been one of her favorite books as a child, Sydney was reminded of Lewis Carroll's *Through the Looking-Glass*. She felt like she was in a crazy world where everything was backward, where people asked the questions they should have been answering, and people's roles—hers, most importantly—were suddenly and irrevocably reversed.

"I'm not sure what you mean," Sydney said, her voice sounding odd and tinny to her own ears after so many hours of not speaking to anyone. "I was really hoping *you* were going to tell me what I was doing here, to tell you the truth."

Sloane raised his eyebrows slightly but said nothing. Then he leaned forward and began again, his voice sounding huskier and more intense.

"Sydney, I know we haven't been working together long," Sloane said. "Still, I'd like to think that we've developed some sort of rapport in our brief time together."

Now it was time for Sydney to raise her eyebrows—it was all she could do not to roll her eyes at her handler. *Rapport?* she thought. *If we have such great rapport, what have I been doing cooling my heels in some basement cell for God knows how long?*

"You seem skeptical," Sloane continued. "And there's no reason for you to believe me when I tell you that I am concerned for you. But I *am* concerned for you, Sydney."

Great, Sydney thought. *But if this is the way you show your concern, I'd hate to see what you do to people who actually make you mad!*

"Which is why," Sloane finally finished, briefly rubbing the bridge of his nose with his fingers, "I want you to believe me when I tell you that the sooner you're honest with me, the more I can help you."

Sydney sat there, stunned. *Well, let's sum up,* she thought. *First I retrieved the documents you asked for in record time. Then you blindfolded and handcuffed me and had me placed in some unknown location, with no human contact except two guys who both look like the Incredible Hulk.*

What Sydney said aloud came out in a much more controlled manner.

"I'm confused," she said honestly. "I have no idea why I'm here. I certainly have no information. I'm waiting for you to tell me what's going on, not the other way around."

Sloane's nostrils flared. An angry mask covered his features and was then immediately replaced by his usual noncommittal expression. For Sydney, though, that brief glimpse of anger had been enough to send a chill of fear down her spine. She'd never seen Sloane angry. He reached into his jacket and pulled out a small digital tape recorder.

"This conversation was intercepted by Interpol almost thirty-six hours ago," Sloane said. He pressed Play and pushed the tape recorder into the center of the table. "Maybe you can tell us something about it."

Immediately, a high female voice issued from the small speaker.

"The seeds are planted," the voice said. "Crocuses are coming up all over."

A male voice answered. "Do you think there's going to be rain tomorrow?"

The female didn't hesitate. "Oh, most definitely," she said. "A thunderstorm, I hope."

Sloane reached across and shut off the player. He placed both hands flat on the table. "Anyone you know?" he asked.

Sydney shook her head, refusing to believe what she'd heard. But it was impossible to deny. All the cadences, the pauses—the very *timbre* of the voice—were as familiar to her as her most comfortable pair of old shoes. That voice could only belong to one person.

"It—it—it sounds like me," Sydney finally got out. She was incredulous. Had she been having bizarre conversations about gardening with some stranger in her sleep? "A *lot* like me," she finally allowed.

Sloane smiled the deep, satisfied smile of someone who'd just gotten up from a full, delicious meal.

"Yes, that's what our analysts thought too," Sloane said. "And you know what? Voiceprint technology confirms that it is, in fact, you."

But I never had any such conversation! Sydney

thought wildly. *I don't even know what those people are talking about!*

Taking a deep breath, she tried to transmit that information to Sloane in a voice much calmer than the scream in her brain.

"Sir," she began, "not only is that not me on the tape, I still have no idea what this entire situation is all about."

The anger that had flashed across Sloane's face earlier returned—this time, to stay. "I'm trying to help you, Sydney," he said, rising and shaking his head. "But you're not making it very easy for me."

Sydney's head was spinning. Didn't Sloane know that such recordings could be faked?

But who would fake a recording of my voice? Sydney asked herself, then, hoping against hope, added, *Could it be part of the test?*

What happened next destroyed any of Sydney's hopes that the previous few days had been some kind of an elaborate hoax designed to rattle junior agents. Sloane walked over to a monitor set up in the corner, pressed a button, and regarded the flickering screen. His back to Sydney, he asked another ominous question.

"I suppose you have no idea what this is about either?"

If Sydney hadn't seen the tape with her own

eyes, she never would have believed it. But what was unfolding in front of her was undeniable.

The tape was grainy, with a digital readout of the time and date in the corner. It was a typical security tape, the kind Sydney had examined hundreds of times in her work.

The only difference was that this time, she was on it.

Sydney recognized the location very well. There she was, in the archives museum in Berlin, paging through the files in the basement office.

If Sydney had been giving the tape only a cursory examination, she would have thought this was simply all a mistake of Noah's or Lucy's—that the security feed had not been disabled after all, and that this was the transmission of her episode in Berlin.

But as she looked more closely, she knew she'd never seen the outfit she was wearing on the tape—from the grainy look of it, loose cargo pants, a black turtleneck, and a wool hat pulled low on her forehead. Also, the time of day was all wrong. When she had been in the basement room, light had been coming through a side window. In this tape, the room was dark and the lights were on. And she would never have taken the documents and stuffed them into her pocket—as the woman on the screen was doing.

A woman who looked a lot like Sydney.

"We've received intelligence that leads us to believe that the documents we were looking for—the documents that were missing from your scans on our mission in Berlin, incidentally—are now in the hands of K-Directorate." Sloane glowered.

Sydney couldn't speak. She was still mesmerized by the image that was now repeating in an endless loop. The woman entered through the side window, scrambled over to the table, and pulled the Radikovitch file apart. Then she stuffed a paper or two in her voluminous pockets, jumped onto the table, and exited from the still-open window into what looked like pouring rain.

"Those aren't my clothes and it . . . it was daytime when I was there," Sydney said with as much confidence as she could muster. She stood up and walked over to the screen. "It's a fake."

"Graham and Lucy have been over the tape now at least a hundred times," Sloane said. "They are convinced it is you."

Sydney looked at Sloane and waited until his eyes turned from the flickering screen and met hers again. She didn't know how it had been done, but she knew very well that it wasn't her on the tape. "They're wrong," she said.

"When SD-6's computers picked up the transmission, at first we thought it was a tape of your mission," Sloane said. "But it appears you made a deal with K-Directorate, and they're selling you out." He made a clucking noise. "Sydney, didn't you know Anna Espinosa hates you? There's no way she wouldn't use your treachery as an opportunity to get you, no way she could ever trust you enough to let you work as a double agent for K-Directorate after what she's been through with you."

Sydney walked back over to the table and slammed her hands down on it. "I'm not working for Anna Espinosa!" she said, getting a sour taste on her tongue even as the name passed her lips.

Sloane smiled—a slow, dangerous smile. "You may be clever, but you're not clever enough to fight me, Sydney. And once we find the wire transfer or bank account with the monies K-Directorate paid you, it's over."

Sydney slumped into her chair again. It was becoming clear to her now that whoever had manufactured her voice on the phone and then her image on the Berlin tape could have easily also arranged for a sizable store of money in some Swiss bank on her behalf.

One thing was clear: she was dealing with an enemy whose resources staggered and totally eclipsed her own—especially those she had available from an empty jail cell.

"There's only one thing I can say," Sydney said. "It's not true, and I'm going to prove that it's not true."

But Sloane wasn't going for it. "That's all very well, Agent Bristow, but I can't have a rogue agent in my custody. Tomorrow, I'm going upstairs."

For a minute, Sydney thought he literally meant upstairs, as in above the room where they were sitting. But that was just her denial working. In another half a second, it was clear what was going on. If Sydney didn't produce some of the information Sloane wanted, he was going to give her over to the big boys at the CIA for arrest.

Sydney felt a moment of panic. What did this mean for her future? Endless debriefings? Life in a jail cell?

Or did former SD-6 agents go someplace else . . . someplace that wasn't even as good as a jail cell?

8

THE FOLLOWING MORNING, THE knock on the door came earlier than Sydney expected.

She had spent the night completely unable to sleep, tossing and turning. *I should have escaped when I had the chance,* she thought, trying to keep her desperation from turning into a gusher of full-fledged, unstoppable tears. *Now there's no way I'm going to escape the grand jury . . . and no way I'm ever going to figure out who's setting me up.*

At the close of her meeting with Sloane, he had been very clear about what was going to happen if Sydney, as he put it, refused to cooperate: she would be removed to federal prison, where she would await trial. Because the evidence against her was so clear and irrefutable, the judgment would be swift and—Sloane was particularly clear on this point—"of the highest order," punitively speaking.

"If you tell me who you're working for, Sydney, I can help you," Sloane kept saying. "But if you refuse to divulge anything, you're going to leave me with no choice but to turn you over to the authorities."

Hearing the man she'd trusted throughout her career at SD-6 talk about ending that career, Sydney felt like she was trying to swallow a hard, sticky baseball. Still, there was no choice but to tell the truth—and continue to tell it, hoping that someone would eventually listen and believe.

"I can't explain any of these tapes except to tell you that I had no involvement in selling information to any enemy agency, that I am loyal to SD-6, and that you must pursue another avenue in order to find out what has happened here," Sydney repeated thickly.

Anger had darkened Arvin Sloane's face like a cloud passing over the sun. Sydney knew it was over. And she was frightened.

I'm going to have to call my dad, Sydney thought as they led her back to the cell. *But how can*

*he help me? He doesn't know any lawyers. SD-6
agents are allowed to get lawyers, right?*

She thought of the cold, distant man with
whom she'd had as little contact as possible as soon
as she'd left home and started at UCLA. She
thought of how, even though they'd never been
close, her father had been pursuing more contact
with her over the past year—contact that gave her
hope that he wouldn't abandon her now.

*Let's just hope Dad does knows a lawyer. A
really good lawyer,* Sydney thought.

After a short interval in the cell, just like a pris-
oner awaiting an execution, Sydney was allowed to
take a shower—even if it was in a bare, galvanized
stall that resembled an empty water tank more than
any civilized bathroom. The meal that followed was a
dry steak, rubbery potatoes, and slightly burned peas.

As she tried unsuccessfully to settle down to
sleep, two questions would not leave her alone. The
first was, simply, what in the world had they told
Francie about her missing roommate, who had now
been AWOL for at least five days? And the second
was, who was responsible for the current scenario
in which Sydney was being brought down by a
crime she didn't commit?

She knew that nothing would be resolved

until she could figure out the answer to the second question.

Sydney was pretty sure she knew the answer to the first one. Just like the analysts at SD-6 had been able to send a stream of correspondence that established Sydney as Ilsa Tannenhaus to a Berlin museum, they could send an e-mail to Francie that happily told her that her roomie would be away on her "business trip" a few days extra.

And with the number of times I've traveled for SD-6 over the past year, she wouldn't blink twice at a note like that, Sydney realized. If need be, they could even use whatever technology had been used to put Sydney's voice in that taped phone conversation Sloane had played for her to put some kind of chirpy, happy message on the answering machine for Francie to conveniently pick up whenever she quit cursing Sydney out for working so much.

Which led her directly to the second question. Who had put her voice on that tape—and her body in Berlin an entire day earlier than she'd actually been there?

It went without saying, Sydney reasoned, that whoever had done so was significantly involved with SD-6. It would have been too much of a co-incidence for someone to place Sydney somewhere stealing documents she was going to scan a day later.

But maybe that means it really was *a coincidence*, Sydney thought. *After all, why should I steal something twice? Couldn't I just take whatever documents I'm getting for SD-6 and then transfer them to whatever enemy body I'm supposedly working for?*

But even as she thought it, Sydney knew that theory wouldn't hold water. *Because time is money,* Sydney thought. *SD-6 wanted these Radikovitch documents first so that they could find the plans for the gun—if they even existed at all—first. Whoever stole the real ones—and planted an image of me at the scene doing it instead—not only wanted to get to the documents first, they wanted to make sure they had someone else doing it.*

But how did they plant that image of me? Sydney asked herself, her head spinning. *Maybe I really did steal those documents. Maybe I did have that conversation. Maybe I should just turn myself in to Sloane—not for being guilty, but for being crazy.*

Sydney knew there was no way she was going to do anything of the kind. Her curiosity—and her determination—were much stronger, as always, than her desire to quit.

That brought her back to her thinking about

SD-6. She kept asking herself who had the knowledge—and the power—to pull off something like the bulldozer that was running through the remnants of her old life as the hours ticked by.

The possible players, Sydney reasoned, were few. There was Sloane, but what reason did he have to bring Sydney down? *Don't forget what happened with Wilson, though,* Sydney reminded herself. The year before, she'd thought that her handler was more solid than the granite face she'd scaled at the SD training camp. Turned out he'd been working for the enemy all along. *Maybe Sloane isn't on your side either,* she reminded herself.

But what possible reason would Sloane have for framing Sydney? And what could he possibly gain by doing so? All she'd ever done was produce good work for him—in taking her out, Sloane would be more than cutting off his nose to spite his face.

Anyway, Sloane's in charge. He doesn't need any excuses or reasons to kill me. If he wanted me to be dead, I'd just be dead.

Which led Sydney to another thought. Whoever was doing this, Sydney realized, hadn't wanted to kill Sydney.

They'd wanted SD-6 to do it for them.

Who could be so cowardly as to use her own organization against her?

And who had the technological resources to do it?

As soon as Sydney asked the question, it answered itself. There was only one person so despicable, so devious, as to try to off Sydney in a sophisticated tangle that would have made Sherlock Holmes flip over in his grave.

Anna Espinosa of K-Directorate.

Realizing who was responsible—the only person who *could* be responsible—for her current circumstances filled Sydney with a righteous anger that made tears start in her eyes and her jaw tremble. And that anger changed to a cold fear when she realized that, however Anna had managed to bring this off, she almost certainly had not been working alone.

Which left Sydney back at square one—still figuring out who at SD-6 had both reason and opportunity to have betrayed her so horribly.

There was Lucy, who, as a new technological consultant, certainly might have the gizmo expertise to pull something like this off. Still, she was new, and she didn't have any reason to bring Sydney down, or enough institutional knowledge to know how to go about it.

But if she's working with Espinosa, she'd be nearly unstoppable, Sydney reminded herself.

There were two possible players: Agent Mirofsky and, as much as Sydney hated to consider it, Noah. Her experience with Wilson had taught her that she couldn't trust even the people closest to her—even those that had always given her every reason to depend on them absolutely.

If it's Noah who betrayed me, Sydney thought, *then—despite all that's happened between us—I really never knew him at all.*

It was an extremely disquieting thought, and Sydney found that even considering it was physically and mentally almost unbearable.

But Noah had saved Sydney's life too many times for her to believe that he'd ever do anything to harm her, Sydney reasoned, glad to lift her thoughts out of the black sewer of doubt. He was her partner—and, she sometimes thought, the closest she was ever going to come to a boyfriend. The thought of him doing anything like this was absurd. Even if he had opportunity, he lacked the one thing Sydney's considerable analytical training had led her to look for in every instance when seeking the perpetrator of a crime.

Motive.

And that leaves Anya Mirofsky, Sydney thought, turning on the uncomfortable bunk once more in an effort to find out if the unforgiving slats yielded at least one pain-free position. *Sloane's new protégée.*

And—just like that—Sydney realized she'd found her motive.

Mirofsky must be angling for a higher position in SD-6, she thought, the theory gaining credence even as the knots in her muscles tightened from the torturous bed. *And for some reason, she thinks she's got to get me out of the way in order to succeed.*

Suddenly, Sydney remembered their brief interlude in the hallway, cursing herself for having forgotten it for these past two days she'd been imprisoned. At the time, she'd thought Mirofsky was just trying to psych her out, bullying the junior agent into knowing her place whether she was the key operator on the mission or not.

But she was planting a bug, Sydney realized. *A bug that would give her enough of my voice to create any message she wanted. Hell, she could probably make a tape of me reading the Declaration of Independence if she wanted to!*

The exact details of how Mirofsky had accomplished all this didn't matter to Sydney. She felt herself flushing at how long it had taken for her to put it together at all.

Still, I can't take this to Sloane without any proof, Sydney thought. *There's no reason for him to believe me. It's just going to seem as if I'm pointing fingers at anyone I can at this point.*

And how was she going to escape and *find* that proof when Sloane was giving her over to his superiors in the morning? It was hopeless.

As much as she hated to admit it, one part of her was disappointed that Noah hadn't been in the picture at all thus far. Had he just heard what was going on through the grapevine and given up on her completely? Didn't he know she would never, ever do anything so despicable and lowly as sell secrets to the enemy?

Maybe I was being too optimistic about us, Sydney thought. *Maybe all that distance between Noah and me that I thought was because of our life in SD-6 was just that—distance.*

Sydney turned over in the bed again. There was a loud creak. For a moment, she thought nothing of it, but then, like a yellow blade, a swath of light was cutting across her concrete floor. The door was opening.

Sydney sat up. *Noah!* He'd figured some way to come get her after all. Now everything would be okay—they would solve this thing together.

But the figure who appeared in the door was short, spiky-haired, and almost unfamiliar to Sydney. It took a moment before her features swam into focus.

It was Lucy.

"C'mon," Lucy whispered, holding the door wide open. "There isn't a lot of time."

* * *

Driving hell-bent for leather through downtown L.A., Lucy was bringing Sydney up to speed *and* saving her life—that is, Sydney thought, if she didn't kill them both first.

Careening around a corner, Lucy stuck a cigarette in her mouth, lit it, and puffed away, all while continuing to jabber at Sydney. Sydney caught the words *Mirofsky, K-Directorate, Radikovitch,* and *payoff* in one crammed-together stream of information. Lucy was talking so fast it was impossible to follow her—or maybe, Sydney thought, she'd just lost the ability to understand other human beings during her time in the cell.

"Wait, wait, slow down," Sydney said. "You're losing me, and I want to understand this, believe me!"

Lucy sighed, ditching the cigarette butt out the window and almost simultaneously lighting a new one. "You'll understand better when I get you to the warehouse."

But even though Sydney was incredibly grateful for being sprung out of SD-6's prison, she was sick of being out of the loop. "I don't mean to sound rude," Sydney said. "But if someone doesn't tell me what's going on soon, I'm going to scream."

Physically, Sydney was feeling like she was reaching her breaking point. When Lucy had pulled her out the door of her cell ten minutes earlier, she'd expected to have to fight—or at least gently explain—something to the two goons who'd been guarding her ever since she got off the plane at Berlin.

But the hallway outside her cell had been empty. "What the . . . ," Sydney had said. "There's no time!" Lucy interjected.

Before she knew it, they were out of the hallway, up a back staircase, and walking through the lobby of some large, anonymous hotel in downtown L.A. *One of SD-6's many haunts,* Sydney had thought, making a mental note of the location.

Lucy, who had shifted into a higher gear as they passed through an industrial district, was finally slowing down. She flashed Sydney a pitying look. "Shhh," she said. "This is all going to be over soon, and I promise you, you'll know everything there is to know."

But Sydney couldn't stop herself from asking more questions. "Is Noah there?" she asked. "Was it Agent Mirofsky?"

Lucy pulled the car in front of a spectacularly

beat-up looking warehouse—one that, to Sydney, looked like it hadn't been in operation since at least the 1950s. "In here," she said, gesturing Sydney through a battered steel door into a vast, empty factory floor with a huge computer on a table in the far corner.

Lucy took a seat at the table and began to plink away at the keyboard faster than even Sydney could follow. In a moment, an illustration of a human female body came up on the screen, outlined in glowing green.

"Look familiar?" Lucy asked.

To Sydney, it looked just like one of the average female body illustrations you could find in any medical textbook or the encyclopedia. "Um . . . not really," Sydney said. What could this have to do with what was going on?

Lucy turned to face Sydney. "Look again," she said.

Sydney leaned closer. True, it was a lot like the body she saw in the mirror after she went swimming or got out of the shower. Then again, you saw her type of slim, athletic build all over L.A.

"I guess it looks a little like me," Sydney admitted. "But they take a body scan of me every time I enter SD-6. They take one of all of us, you know that. Is that what this is?"

"Not exactly," Lucy said. "Listen, you know how in video games they can take a scan of a human figure, than animate it using markers on a real, live moving person?"

"Sort of," Sydney said. Then it suddenly clicked. "Is this how they put me on that tape?" she asked.

Lucy shook her head. "I went over those tapes with Graham a million times, and we can't figure out how anyone could have done it. I mean, Hollywood can make it *look* like someone's there, but the technology doesn't exist yet to do the kind of thing that's happened here."

Sydney's heart fell. "But if the technology doesn't exist, then we haven't solved anything, right?"

Lucy shook her head. "Maybe not," she said. "I don't know what to tell you."

Sydney shook her head, literally not believing what she was hearing. "Lucy, I don't understand," she said. "You help me escape from a jail cell, you bring me to this remote location, you show me these random images . . ."

Even in her fatigue, Sydney could see that Lucy's eyes were glittering strangely. Slowly, Sydney began to draw back. "This is part of it, isn't it?" she whispered.

Lucy was grinding another butt into the heap already in the huge black ashtray on the computer desk. "Sydney," she said, turning to her. "You're a very smart girl. Why don't you tell me?"

Sydney was already looking around the empty floor for a weapon, and something unreadable passed across Lucy's face. Sydney saw her glance—quickly—at her watch.

"What are you waiting for?" Sydney asked. Without wasting any more time, she grabbed Lucy and placed her in a simple headlock, drawing her left arm upward in what she knew had to be an incredibly painful position.

"What's happening here?" Sydney asked, forcing the now yelping Lucy to her feet. "Who are you working for?"

"That's right, Sydney," Lucy muttered, twisting violently. "Get it out—get it all out."

Suddenly, Sydney heard the *thwock-thwock-thwock* of a helicopter overhead.

"It's happening," Lucy murmured. Then she began screaming bloody murder. "Help! Help! We're in here! Somebody, please help me!"

Sydney was so agitated that she pulled Lucy even closer, not knowing what the crazy tech consultant was going to do next. "I don't know what kind of game you're playing, Lucy," she said, struggling to keep a grip on the flailing, petite blonde, "but you better end it right now, or I'll break your arm."

That only caused Lucy to begin laughing maniacally. "Do whatever you want, you idiot," she said, using the sheer force of her body weight to yank Sydney toward the steel door they'd come in minutes before. "Break both of them if you want!"

Sydney wanted to step back, but now Lucy had a strong grip on her lower arms, her nails digging into Sydney's skin as she raked it again and again. Sydney was about to coldcock her when she heard a loud banging at the door.

"Agent Bristow, give up your hostage!" she heard a slightly accented voice say over a loudspeaker. "We can end this peacefully!"

The voice startled Sydney so that she dropped her headlock on Lucy completely. *Hostage?* she thought. *What the hell is Anya Mirofsky talking about?*

She didn't know what was going on with the babbling Lucy, but it was clear enough what was happening outside. SD-6 was there in full force, and they somehow had the idea that Sydney Bristow was holding the gentle Lucy as a hostage.

I know what's going on, Sydney suddenly realized. *Mirofsky and Lucy are working together.*

When she comes in here, Mirofsky's going to shoot me; it's going to look like self-defense, I'm going to be dead, and then Mirofsky and Lucy are going to take a huge payoff from Anna Espinosa for a job well done.

Sydney had to admit that it was a brilliant plan. Working together, Anya and Lucy could easily convince SD-6 that Sydney, already on the run, had kidnapped Lucy as protection, and that she would shoot anyone to save herself, to get out, to go underground.

And Sydney would no longer be alive to let them know that it was all a lie.

But one thing was clear: Sydney wasn't going to let this lie come to its obvious and violent conclusion. There was no way she was going to play along.

Stepping as far away from Lucy as she could manage while still maintaining a clear view of the door, Sydney readied her voice to shout so that she could be heard over the huge whooping thrum of the helicopter. *If I can just screw up their story,* Sydney thought, *they won't be able to shoot me right away.*

"Agent Mirofsky, there's no hostage situation here," Sydney yelled. "I repeat: there's *no hostage situation.* I am unarmed, and I am prepared to come out and surrender peacefully!"

But it was no use. It was clear that no one would be able to hear her over the blades of the SD-6 helicopter—in which Arvin Sloane, Sydney knew, probably sat calmly regarding the proceedings.

There was only one thing to do—walk out and take her chances.

As she began to walk toward the door, Sydney reasoned that, even though she was currently considered a fugitive and a kidnapper, if she walked out with her hands up, there was a fifty-fifty chance that she wouldn't be shot on sight. If she stayed inside with someone SD-6 considered a potential hostage—especially one of their own—there was no telling what could happen.

And just being shot, Sydney thought, raising her hands, *would frankly be a step up at this point.*

But as she moved toward the door, Lucy tackled her from behind.

"Ooof!" she grunted as they hit the rock-hard floor together. Sydney just had a second to throw her hand in front of her mouth and keep her jaw from shattering against the dirty, blasted concrete.

She had to get away from Lucy—and quickly, so her plan could still be put into operation. Using the instincts that had been honed throughout more than a year of hard SD-6 training, Sydney flipped Lucy over easily and slapped her twice across the face. She'd considered knocking her out and decided not to—whatever happened next, she wanted Lucy to be conscious for the proceedings. *I've got to be able to make her talk,* Sydney thought wildly, grabbing Lucy by the hair and yanking her, once again, to a yelping, jabbering standing position, ready to shove her away and make a break for the door. *She's got to explain what's going on to SD-6, to Arvin Sloane, to everybody—whether she likes it or not.*

"Agent Bristow! Stand down now!"

Sydney looked up. Agent Mirofsky stood in the door, her gun trained on Sydney's forehead, where Sydney could almost feel the red dot she knew currently flickered there from the scope on Mirofsky's weapon.

Sydney stuttered in her desperation. "Agent M-Mirofsky, d-don't do it! I know what's going on here! Don't do it or you'll regret it, I swear!"

Slowly, she raised her hands. Lucy scrambled off to the side, still screaming. Sydney knew these next few seconds were critical, and she used the only weapon left to her. She began to bluff.

"Agent Mirofsky, I have proof of your involvement in this scheme, and you will go down for it," Sydney said, trying to inject the calm note of confidence she always heard in Noah's voice whenever they were in a tight spot together. "Rest assured, the higher-ups in the CIA are well aware of your actions in this matter, and if you shoot me, you'll only be putting the nail in your own coffin."

Sydney had expected Mirofsky's lip to curl in scorn as it had that long-ago day at the meeting. But despite the fact that she was holding a gun, she was only giving Sydney a look of deep confusion.

And she still hadn't lowered the gun one millimeter.

"Agent Bristow, you are the only one who is going to be arrested today," Agent Mirofsky said. Sydney raised her hands even higher, willing some other agent to burst into the room behind Mirofsky. If there were any other witnesses, she would be safe. But as long as she was left alone with Lucy and Mirofsky, she had zero chance of survival.

Unless she could escape out the back door.

Sydney snuck a quick look at the rear of the warehouse. Lucy had disappeared into the shadows. Behind her stretched the empty floor.

Sydney turned back, realizing she'd tipped Agent Mirofsky off. Mirofsky had begun her approach—the

approach Sydney herself had used many times: slow
enough not to rattle the perpetrator, but fast enough
that he or she had no time to escape.

In that second, Sydney decided that whatever
happened, her chances were better if she ran. She
turned to do just that and found herself facing Lucy,
who was standing directly in the center of the warehouse floor, pointing a sleek handgun directly at
Sydney.

She was trapped.

Lucy cocked her pistol. "I was hoping you
would do this for me," she said.

Sydney felt sick. Had Mirofsky and Lucy
drawn straws to determine who would get the
pleasure of executing Sydney in cold blood?

Lucy fired the gun.

In that moment, Sydney's entire being seized.
The first face she saw was her mother's—lingering
over her as it had those many years before when
she'd tucked her in for bed, singing songs to help
her get to sleep. Then her father's face swam before
her, not filled with admonishment but kind and
gentle, as she'd rarely seen it in real life. Then she
saw Francie, laughing and talking and calling to
her, standing in the middle of the quad with her
hands outstretched.

And then she realized she hadn't been shot at all.

Trembling and unable to utter a sound, Sydney turned around. Anya Mirofsky lay on the ground in a pool of blood, her hand outstretched, still clutching the gun.

Sydney turned back to Lucy. "You shot Mirofsky," she said, still not believing what had occurred.

"No, I didn't," Lucy said. She walked over to the still-shocked Sydney, shoved the gun in her hand, and, before Sydney could stop her, forced Sydney to fire off another round into Anya's lifeless body.

Then, grinning, Lucy pulled off a set of almost invisible, webbed gloves and crammed them in her mouth, chewing happily. She pointed at Sydney and wagged her finger gently, like a schoolteacher scolding a naughty child.

"You did," Lucy said.

9

THE NEXT TWENTY MINUTES passed in a blur.

Immediately after Lucy shoved the still-hot gun in Sydney's hands and fired it, Sydney dropped it like a radioactive ball, staring at Lucy in shock. But it was too late.

Suddenly, what had happened was all too clear.

Not only have I been framed for stealing documents and selling them to K-Directorate, Sydney thought, backing away from Lucy in horror. *Now SD-6 will come in here and think that, while holding Lucy hostage, I shot Agent Mirofsky.*

The gun rested on the concrete floor. Sydney

saw, with a sick sense of irony, that it had landed and spun around to face precisely in her direction.

For the first time in her life, Sydney understood what it was to feel completely hopeless. She'd taken on the enemies of SD-6 countless times and had not been afraid. She'd beaten up men twice her size and broken into terrorist facilities controlled and guarded by enough men holding guns to form a small army. But she'd never fought her home organization—the people who had trained her.

And she didn't know what to do now that they thought she was the enemy.

Okay, Sydney, think, she said. *You've got exactly ten seconds before the rest of SD-6 comes in here after you.*

So Sydney decided something. If SD-6 was going to treat her like a criminal, she was going to have to start thinking like one.

Like the greatest criminal mastermind who ever lived, Sydney thought, knowing that she simply didn't have it in her. *Even though I've spent my entire life thinking in completely the opposite way.*

Well, the first step was obvious. If she was a hostage-taker, she might as well take her hostage.

Lucy had backed up a few feet, waiting, with Sydney, for the SD-6 muscle to follow in Agent Mirofsky's path. Scooping the gun up off the floor,

Sydney vaulted across the room, grabbed Lucy, and held the gun to her head.

"If I'm going down, you're going down with me," Sydney said in Lucy's ear.

But Lucy was unmoved. "You'll be dead before you can open your mouth," she said. "Think about it, Sydney—you've just killed Agent Mirofsky, and now you're about to kill me. The SD-6 sharpshooters will get you before you can do anything."

There was nothing to say, Sydney realized. It was totally true.

But not if I give up my hostage first, Sydney suddenly thought.

Outside, Sydney could hear the screech of a car pulling up, then another. There were the sounds of commotion and shouting. It was clear what was happening. They were getting ready to break in, and Sydney's time was running out.

Pushing Lucy out in front of her toward the sunlit open door, Sydney crouched slightly, making sure her head was well behind Lucy's spiky hair. As they walked around Anya, Sydney willed herself not to look down and uttered a silent prayer and apology for the fallen agent.

I'm sorry, Agent Mirofsky, Sydney thought. *I had the wrong person. But I have the right one now.*

She gave an extra jab with the gun at Lucy's temple for emphasis.

"I hope you enjoy being dead," Lucy spat. "Because that's what you're going to be in exactly five seconds."

"Shut up and raise your hands," Sydney said. When Lucy didn't move, Sydney jabbed her in the kidney, which she knew to be the most painful, crippling place on the torso to hit. Lucy's hands went up.

Here goes, Sydney thought.

Holding her breath, Sydney collected all her strength and shoved Lucy as hard as she could through the open door into what she knew would be a waiting crowd of agents. Next, she took the gun, laid it on the cold concrete, and shoved it out across the asphalt like a hockey puck. She couldn't look.

And then, over the *thwock-thwock-thwock* of the helicopter blades, it came.

"Release the hostage and come out with your hands up," a voice said over the loudspeaker. It was Arvin Sloane's.

Closing her eyes, Sydney took several deep breaths, trying to still the hot, aching trembling that had overtaken all of her limbs, as if she were suffering from a terrible fever. She thrust her hands up, preparing herself for whatever waited for her outside. She didn't know if she would be shot immediately or if she would be returned to the prison to await her execution. All she knew was that her life as she knew it was over.

Sydney opened her eyes and closed them, and a tear ran down each cheek. She wiped at them hurriedly. She didn't want to go out looking humiliated and beaten. She wanted to step out with pride, standing straight, knowing the truth, even if no one else did. It didn't matter that she had finally come to the end of the road, that she had found the one dead end from which she couldn't escape. All that mattered was that she knew she was innocent—and that she'd done good work all the months she'd been in service with SD-6.

Sydney suddenly thought back to a little over a year before, when she'd been a gawky freshman, fiercely running around the track, trying to find herself in the vastness of UCLA. Back then, the university had seemed as big and scary a world as she ever could have imagined.

I had no idea, Sydney thought bitterly. *No idea at all.*

What if, when SD-6 had come for her, she'd simply said no? How different would her life be now?

Well, for one, I'd probably be sitting eating a

pizza with Francie instead of facing a wall of high-powered assault rifles, Sydney thought, furiously swiping away at another round of tears. *And now I'm going to have to say good-bye to Francie, and she's never even going to know what happened to me.*

She knew that SD-6 would be able to take care of that just like they'd take care of her.

But Sydney knew she had no more time to think, to simply stand there. If she didn't walk out with her hands up immediately, SD-6 would be coming in to get her.

Sydney took a breath and passed through the door into the open air.

Her immediate sensation was of a wall of black rushing up to meet her. The sunlight bounced off a row of unmarked cars. A row of officers holding shiny guns. But not pointed at her. *Not pointed at her.*

Noah Hicks was running toward the door, toward the center of the circle, and he caught Sydney as she fell into a faint.

"Sydney, Sydney!" Noah yelled, crushing her face against his jacket in a fierce embrace. "Thank *God* you're all right."

* * *

"But how did you finally figure out what had really happened?" Sydney asked, running a finger through the sand with a glorious feeling of freedom.

She and Noah were sitting on the beach that Sydney had come to think of as their beach, the one they always went to after their missions to talk through what had gone well, what had gone wrong—and what was going on with them.

Noah turned over and took Sydney's hand. "I never had to figure anything out, Syd," he said. "I knew you could never have done what SD-6 thought you did, no matter *what* was on that tape. It was just a matter of figuring out who really had."

Sydney and Noah had been in debriefings until late afternoon, as SD-6 had pieced the situation together.

"Well, I really appreciate your getting suspended for me," Sydney said, squeezing Noah's hand back, trying to transmit the depth of her affection and gratefulness.

Noah looked deep into her eyes, letting a moment of silence lengthen. "I would have done a lot more than that for you, Sydney," he said finally, leaning in to place a light kiss on her lips.

As Sydney had learned, Noah had been taken off the case immediately after their return to Berlin, and he and Lucy had been subjected to a grueling series of debriefings to figure out if they too had been involved in what was being touted as one of the worst betrayals in SD-6's history.

"But I knew that Arvin was jumping to conclusions, and that if Graham just kept examining the material, we'd finally figure out what had really happened," Noah had told Sydney as soon as they had found a moment together.

Graham's breakthrough had come just at the moment of crisis, when Sydney, lured away by Lucy, was believed to have masterminded her own escape, taking Lucy as a hostage for insurance.

"In fact," Noah explained now, "she was just using the animation technology on the SD-6 feed."

"Does that mean that if they had just checked inside the cell, those stupid goons would have seen that I was there?" Sydney asked, her frustration threatening to make tears break out yet again.

Noah drew Sydney closer to him, resting his arm over her shoulder as they gazed out over the ocean. "Well, Arvin uses those guys for SD-6 muscle," he said. "Not brains."

Sydney laughed. "Well, I'm just glad we had your brains instead," she said, and then realized, with a glad rush, that it was the first time she'd had something to laugh about in days.

As Noah explained—and as Sydney had

learned in the debriefing—Noah had suspected Anya Mirofsky was crooked from the beginning. That, Sydney now was glad to understand, had explained Noah's interest in the new agent—not her long legs or her mesmerizing green eyes.

"I tried to tell Arvin that I thought we needed to check her out more, but he wouldn't listen," Noah said. "So I guess our secret's out."

Sydney smiled. "Well, if we had to let out the truth about our relationship to save my life, then that's worth it to me."

Noah gave a half smile. "I still don't know how he found out about it," he said. "I wish I could figure it out—I'm always pretty cold to you in the office."

Sydney laughed again, glad to have Noah finally admit something she'd suspected all along, though the thought that Noah was just playing hot and cold with her had also crossed her mind.

"Well, it's not like I'm exactly leaping all over you trying to kiss you during staff meetings either," Sydney said.

Noah kissed the top of her head. "At this point, you could kiss me on Arvin Sloane's desk and I wouldn't mind," he said. "I'm just so glad I was able to save you before it was too late."

What Graham had finally been able to glean from the tapes that appeared to show Sydney stealing documents from the Berlin museum had been staggering. For the longest time, the dogged technician hadn't been able to figure out how anyone could have tampered with the tapes. The line of Sydney's body and the background had been flawless, he'd told Noah.

But when Lucy had donned a wig and inserted an image of herself into the security feed of Sydney's cell, making it look as if Sydney had escaped, she'd finally made a mistake, Graham saw. He noticed that Sydney had the same expressions as the Sydney on the Berlin tape. The thieves had inserted a new body into the transmissions—but they hadn't inserted a new face.

That was when Noah and Graham realized that Lucy had to be involved. Instead of shutting off the security system's cameras during Sydney's real-life break-in to the Berlin museum, Lucy had simply diverted the feed. The footage she intercepted had provided her with enough images and background to create a proto-Sydney that, with her high-level animation expertise, she could make do almost anything she wanted. And after Sydney revealed during her debriefing that she suspected Anya had tagged her with a bug, the audio aspect of the scam fell into place.

Of course, Anya was dead. Any information she could have brought to the table was lost. Lucy had already spilled all the technological aspects of how she and Anya had achieved their scam, even revealing that the orders to frame Sydney had come from the highest levels in K-Directorate, someone even Lucy had never known by name.

Knowing that someone had created a virtual proxy of her that had fooled even her own team gave Sydney the shivers. Noah, sensing her discomfort, removed his suit jacket and placed it over her shoulders, letting his lips linger on her forehead, her eyes, and finally her mouth.

"I'll never forget what you did for me, Noah," Sydney said, tracing his profile, lit gold by the last traces of the setting sun. "You saved my life."

I can't believe I ever doubted him, Sydney thought, her insides warm with the knowledge she had waited for so long—that Noah cared for her, cared for her enough to risk his life and his career, to say nothing of the wrath of Arvin Sloane. *I can't believe I thought he was interested in Anya. Or that I ever let myself get distracted by that dumb frat guy.*

Noah reached for Sydney's hand, kissed it, and then drew her close to him in one last embrace.

"Sydney, I had no choice but to save your life," Noah said, his lips close to Sydney's ears in a warm whisper. "Because I can't imagine mine without you."

10

You've got to admit this, at least—it was
such a beautiful plan.

Despite what anyone thinks, it started before Paul Ezhersky was killed. Paul's death completely flattened me, but it was what happened
afterward that really destroyed me for good.
It was the breaking point—the last straw in a
long line of last straws with my relationship with
the CIA.

No one ever would have called Paul a funny
guy, exactly, but that was what made him such a
great partner—for once, I got the chance to

show off some of my stuff, to shine a little bit instead of just being benched so often, like all agents the head has designated as "problems." I wonder if the boss knew when he put us together that we would complement each other so well, with Paul being the intellect, analysis, the right-brain half, if you will—and me being the guts, running all on aggression, energy, and pure, good old instinct.

It's true, my relationship with the CIA had never been great. I know I was a problem officer, one of those with a whole filing cabinet of unflattering write-ups and assessments when most others—and I should know, since I've gone through most of the files—get off with something more in the neighborhood of a sheaf the size of a telephone book. But the CIA's a tough place to get fired from once you're in, everybody knows that. Better to have a rogue underfoot than out in the world doing mischief, that's what they say. You've practically got to be xeroxing intelligence and waving it in front of security's face when you walk out the door to get canned from the place.

But more on that later.

Paul and I had worked nearly two years on getting him infiltrated into Chicago's SD-2. That's two years of my life, my friend. Two long years, two years of late nights in the office, eating lukewarm Chinese food and assessing how to best set him up to be tapped by SD-2's head, and after all our hard work paid off and "Paul Riley" was in, making sure he stayed safe. That no one was ever in a position to out him, to put him in danger of losing his life.

Clearly, that worked out well. Not that I'm bitter or anything.

That doesn't even take into account all that I'd lost before Paul—all the things taken away from me when I signed on to the CIA. Let's count them out: there was my fiancé (couldn't take the late nights), my family (only see 'em at Thanksgiving, if I'm lucky), even my dog, Sally (after my fiancé left, I just didn't have time to take care of her anymore).

Yeah, yeah—I know what everyone says. "That's what you signed up for," right? "That's just the nature of the job." "You're serving your country—you're protecting your fellow Americans." You know what's the funniest part? For the longest time, I believed all that crap too.

But I'm getting off topic. I'm letting my anger get the best of me, and if I'm going to finish this—and make no mistake, I am going to finish it—I've got to keep my anger focused, like a ray gun.

Oh, right—the ray gun.

That was all Mirofsky's idea—Anya Mirofsky, the hotshot they brought in from New York to replace Paul after his untimely death. Who cared if she'd brought in some of the biggest heads of k-Directorate? Who cared if she'd been instrumental in breaking up key SD cells forming in Brazil, Tokyo, and Chechnya? I sure didn't. I was much more interested in another problem.

Why no one was investigating Paul's death.

Oh, sure—agents die in the field all the time. It's part of the job, everyone knows that. They prepare you for it with a seminar right before you're brought in, complete with handy jargon that's supposed to make everything okay: <u>The CIA doesn't have the resources to pursue that lead at this juncture. . . . There is no way to protect all field agents at all times. . . . That information is on a need-to-know basis.</u>

Well, I damn sure needed to know.

It's just that I'd never seen anything like the kind of shutdown that occurred after Paul died. Sure, Jack Bristow sent out some little memo saying how sorry the CIA was and how great an agent Paul had been. (<u>Sorry</u>—that's one word for it.) But from the investigation that happened afterward, you would've thought Paul was some old ninety-seven-year-old who had dropped off smiling in his sleep. To say there was no investigation into the circumstances is an understatement. The next day his office was cleared, his file cabinets emptied, all traces of the man gone from the CIA—or all traces of anything accessible by me, his partner.

Not only was there no investigation, it was as if Paul had never existed at all.

I took it upstairs, and there were a whole lot of excuses. They were "satisfied with the information available at this time." They were "pursuing a larger strategy in regards to SO cells" that would be "compromised by further action on this point." They were "unable to authorize further activity in regards to this case."

And suddenly I was moved out of active participation.

I can't say I was surprised. Even if agents aren't tossed wholesale out on the street, the bosses have ways of indicating that they're not too thrilled with something some dumb agent insists on pursuing, even though he's been advised time and time again to let it go.

But if the CIA wasn't going to investigate Paul's death, I damn sure would do it myself. He deserved that much, at least. After all, the CIA had taken him from a wife and a son who loved him, as well as a partner who'd learned—just by watching his cool, calm collected method of working—almost everything he knew from him. In life, he'd given everything to the CIA. In death, he deserved better than some stupid cover-up.

A cover-up that, then, I still didn't understand.

But soon, I would. And I'd be glad for the

fact that, eclipsed by the miraculous and amazing Mirofsky, I'd been moved out of active field service on the team that—along with Paul, of course—I used to basically lead.

So I poked around. I asked questions. It was just that, knowing that the CIA administration wasn't on Paul's side or my side at all, I started to ask them only in private.

I had a lot of lucky breaks, actually. First of all, the bosses didn't move our team off monitoring SD cells all over the country. If they had, I would have never had access to any information on who killed Paul at all. And, as I read through the reams of reports, I realized that everything I'd heard through the grapevine was totally wrong.

We'd all assumed, the whole team, that Stephanie Harling, the SD-2 agent Paul was trying to bring in, was responsible for Paul's death. It would have made sense—who else at that SD training camp had anything to fear from him? That's why I was so infuriated—I knew that we had almost enough to bring down the entire SD-2 facility. That would mean prosecuting them not only for the numerous federal charges of terrorism, weapons proliferation, and criminal conspiracy, but also for one death in particular.

The death of my best friend and partner, Paul Ezhevsky.

But from secret reports that I obtained

from my "authorized" research into SD cells for my team, it seemed that Stephanie Harling hadn't been responsible for that death at all.

Stephanie was a petite blonde, and while witnesses put her on the boat with Paul during the melee, there was another girl who kept cropping up in the reports too. Witnesses described her, unlike Stephanie, as a leggy brunette with, as one particularly dramatic witness put it, "dark, piercing eyes."

Why wasn't there any more info on this mysterious member of another SD cell? Not much to go on for the CIA's hardy team of analysts. From the charts we'd been keeping on the SD configurations, there were only a few possibilities as to her identity. I'd narrowed it down to two junior agents who I knew had been present at the training camp when I had my lucky break. I'll admit it—I don't know how much this plan ever would have taken hold if this hadn't happened.

One day, as I passed Jack Bristow's office, I happened to overhear a computer tech, sitting at Jack's desk, complaining about his computer. "It's dead, Jack," he was saying. "This is what happens when you have the old infrastructure—you've got a mechanics problem, not a technological problem."

Of course, the old guy was his usual no-humor self, not even bothering to cut the poor computer tech a break. "I'm not interested in your theories about the CIA's infrastructure," I heard

Bristow snap. "I need a working computer, and I need it by two o'clock this afternoon. Absolutely no excuses."

Bristow didn't even glance at me as he blew by down the hall on his way to one of those incredibly important high-level, top-secret clearance meetings he's always attending.

But I hung around, having a hunch that this was the break I had been waiting for. After all, I could only find so much intelligence on my own, dipping into files that, truth be told, our team was supposed to be examining anyway. But access to even one file from a senior team member's computer could make all the difference.

So I hung around, waiting for my chance. I knew the procedures of computer replacement at the CIA from having witnessed Paul receive a new laptop years ago from the infamously slow and uncooperative computer services. Oh, it was extremely technical, how the CIA dealt with computer upgrades. First, they transferred all your info to a new machine. Then they took your old machine out back, removed the hard drive, and smashed it to pieces.

Obviously, I had to get ahold of Bristow's hard drive before that happened.

Lurking outside his office near a copier around the hall, I waited until I saw the tech whiz by in the hallway. He'd probably manually erased what was on Bristow's computer before he left it alone, I knew, but I still knew it might be worth it to copy what was there, then run a program I had on my own computer that was capable of picking up any fragments of info that were left over on a supposedly "clean" drive. We used it all the time in the CIA on suspects' computers— I had no compunctions whatsoever about using it on one of our own.

Especially on Jack Bristow— one of the senior officials who'd oh-so-gently prevented me from getting any further with my investigation into Paul's death.

It took less than a minute to copy the drive as I stood there, sweating, ready with the sheaf of useless documents I'd been copying in case anyone came in. And someone did come in, right after I'd popped the disk out of the drive and put it in my pocket. It was the computer tech, and I knew he was looking at me quizzically—wondering, I'm sure, what in the hell I was doing there.

I didn't even look at him. Like the faceless functionary I was, I threw the sheaf of paper on the chair, looked at my watch and walked out. Just another friendly CIA office interaction in a lovely CIA day.

And that moment— when I coolly exited Bristow's office, knowing that the tech had been completely fooled by my yawning, calm demeanor—is when I knew for sure that I'd gone over, that I was no longer using my skills for the CIA but instead was bringing all I had to bear against them. I still didn't know yet where it was going to take me. But I knew I was never coming back.

The tech had done a great job at erasing most of the information. As I sat in my empty apartment, the program scrolling through my disk, trying to recover any data fragments, I almost lost hope. But then the program beeped, asking me if I wanted to view part of a recovered e-mail as a text document.

I clicked Okay, of course, hoping it wasn't simply a memo from food services or one of those alerts with months-old declassified info the CIA was so fond of sending around to everyone.

But what I found was a greater prize than I could have ever dreamed of. It was brief, only a fragment of a memo, but in and of itself it clarified everything, letting me know 1) who had really killed Paul, and 2) why the CIA was not pursuing those responsible.

I wasn't able to see who it was from, but I reached the words "You should be proud of her, Jack. She's an exceptional girl." I was mystified, but only for a second. Suddenly, the last name of one of the junior agents I'd seen on our SD cell breakdowns flashed into my mind.

Sydney Bristow.

Jack Bristow.

They were <u>related.</u>

And from the way whoever had written the memo had chosen his or her words, it seemed a strong possibility that Sydney Bristow was . . . Jack Bristow's daughter?

<u>Sydney Bristow was Jack Bristow's daughter.</u> I still remember how those words bounced around in my brain, like someone had yelled them into an empty cavern, then sat back to hear the diminishing echoes for as long as they lasted.

We all knew that Jack Bristow was the big man on campus in SD world, coming up with intelligence and scoops no one else had any access to. But no one had bothered to inform my lowly team that he had a family connection with the place.

It was pretty easy to see that the blocking of my pursuit of Paul's killer and the mystery junior agent's being Jack's daughter probably were connected. Apparently, keeping that live line of intelligence open was much more important than avenging the death of a CIA agent—just like when prosecutors bargained down the charges against a small fish to get the big fish put in jail.

Well, this time they hadn't counted on another small fish going after that guppy they were protecting.

I had no compunctions whatsoever about killing

scum like Sydney Bristow—I didn't care how valuable whatever intelligence she was obviously feeding her father was to the CIA.

The piece of intelligence I'd picked up was what Paul used to call a chip.

"You don't throw it right into the pot, pal," he'd say, leaning back in his desk chair and folding his hands behind his head, his usual pose when he was giving me the kind of career-building advice he seemed to think a hothead like me desperately needed. "You hold on to it. Hold on to that chip, and then cash it in when you need it most."

If this was a chip, then it was a ten-thousand-dollar one in what had been a five-dollar-ante game.

SD-6 was a cell we had barely managed to penetrate thus far in our campaign for the dissolution of SD's proliferating influence across the globe. (Big coincidence, right?) But at this point, I didn't care about SD-6's evil. All I cared about was solving this riddle—was Sydney Bristow responsible for Paul's death, and, if so what could I do to make sure she paid for it?

Paid for it in full.

And that was when I got in touch with Arvin Sloane. Tit for tat, I told him. You scratch my back, I scratch yours. He thought I was just a dirty agent trying to make a buck to bump up my pathetic federal salary. Actually, I didn't care about the money—though, it's true, SD-6 paid me well. I was just dipping into the SD-6 pool, holding on to my chip, waiting until the opportunity presented itself to get my job done.

There was a reason I didn't kill Sydney Bristow outright, by the way. It wasn't that killing scared me—I'd killed people before in the line of duty when I had to, and I'd felt nothing. And it wasn't that I was scared about having the entire CIA coming after me—if they ever found out, that was. I'd already cut my ties. It was simple: if they didn't care enough about Paul to investigate his death, then I didn't care about them either.

I didn't execute a wholesale assassination of Sydney Bristow because of a kind of egotism on my part. The more I got to know Arvin Sloane over the next couple of months of selling him mainly useless information—and a duplicitous, craven bastard he was—the more I began to think that it would be much, much more satisfying and elegant overall if, instead of killing Sydney myself, I could somehow hatch a plan in which the organization would do away with her for me.

An eye for an eye—and even better than biblical revenge, because Arvin Sloane would do it himself and never see it coming.

Now I wish I'd just killed her outright. Killed her before everything became so messed up.

That was around when Anya got her crackpot scheme to infiltrate SD-6. Oh, I pushed her toward it subtly, sure, I'll admit that. We knew Arvin Sloane was always buying up the work of obscure scientists, particularly those from the Soviet Union. Nobody knew why, but we thought if we could dangle just one of those figures in front of him—totally meaningless, failed, and preposterous as "Radikovitch" was—we might get some interest and be able to place one of our officers inside, maybe even dragging an asset or two in tow.

And—what do you know—Arvin Sloane bit.

I still remember the cheer that went up around the office when we learned that Anya was going to successfully infiltrate SD-6. I was cheering along with everyone else—though for a totally different reason, of course.

Now, finally, I'd be able to put into motion my plan to bring down Sydney Bristow—and finally make her pay for what she'd done to my friend.

Of course, first I had to think of a plan.

I was going along happily, knowing that I'd have months to figure out how to make Anya's presence in SD-6 work for me. That all suddenly changed, however, one day when I was doing a routine check of my server logs. It was same-old same-old for three pages, and then suddenly, the unavoidable truth: Anya Mirofsky had logged onto my computer approximately twenty-six hours before, and she had stayed on, doing God knows what, for a good fourteen minutes.

My first thought was <u>How could she be so stupid?</u>

And my second thought was <u>How much does she know?</u>

Not much, I realized quickly. Of that I was sure. If she'd had any idea of my real relationship with Arvin Sloane, I would have been in federal lockup approximately twenty-five and a half hours before. If she'd even told one of my superiors about her doubts, I realized, I'd be off the case. Perhaps it was only simple curiosity that had led her to poke around in my private—well, the CIA's private—files.

Or the whole Radikovitch lure had nothing to do with the CIA's desire to learn more about SD-6. Maybe it was actually a high-level operation to flush out a mole who was operating inside the CIA.

Me.

And that's when it came to me—a plan that could take care of Mirofsky and Bristow in one fell swoop.

I could call it Two Birds with One Stone. And, in this case, my stone would have to be chosen carefully.

It wasn't too hard to turn to Lucy Stell. When I learned she'd been chosen to go along on the mission, I gave a private cheer. More than once, I'd seen her cut corners, manipulate others, act with the kind of reckless disregard for human life

I'd come to see as standard after Paul's death opened my eyes. I knew that if I dangled all the money Arvin had been paying me over the last few months, she'd come running.

And after she did, the rest was easy. You know what was ironic? Disgusting Lucy and I made a great team. Almost as great a team as Paul and I.

Guess money does make the world go round.

Still, just because Noah Hicks got in the way this time doesn't mean that I won't be able to kill Sydney Bristow.

This time, I'll make sure it gets done right. And I'll do it someplace I've become increasingly familiar with in the last couple of weeks, thanks to my age-defying good looks..

On her own turf.

11

WHEN NOAH FINALLY DROPPED Sydney off at the UCLA campus, dusk had fallen, and the small lights lining all the pathways had just come on.

I can't believe it's been less than a week since I left here, Sydney thought, taking in the regular shouts of students heading to dinner and breathing in the smell of fresh-cut grass like it was the finest perfume. *It felt more like a lifetime . . . and it almost was.*

As she passed in front of the dorm, she saw that the groups of Frisbee players, Hacky Sack experts, and soccer freaks were still out, trying to soak up the last bit of light. She was glad when she couldn't pick Brennan out anywhere among the rambunctious rabble.

I'm so glad I never let anything happen between me and Brennan, Sydney thought, her lips still tingling from Noah's kiss minutes earlier in the car. *I've got to learn to trust more. I never should have doubted my feelings for Noah. And I never should have doubted what we had between us.*

As she walked up the steps, Sydney let her fingers trail along the steel railing, happily thinking of all she and Noah could do now that they wouldn't be forced to hide their relationship for the benefit of SD-6 anymore. There could be dinners, concerts, walks on the beach—perhaps they'd even be able to get lunch after some of those keep-it-quiet SD-6 meetings.

Still no funny business on Sloane's desk, though, Sydney thought, the vision that popped up forcing her to actually smack a hand over her mouth to stifle her laugh.

Sydney knew she was going to need a good cover story for Francie. She'd already determined the basic parameters. It was going to have something to do with an incredibly angry client, an incompetent accountant, and a lost account of fifty-seven dollars that Sydney had been forced to track down. *The fifty-seven dollars is key,* Sydney thought. *That's so ridiculous, Francie will get totally worked up about Credit Dauphine and forget how long I was really gone.*

But when Sydney opened the dorm-room door and hit the light switch, she forgot everything else, including her story.

The bright blue paint she'd watched Francie apply earlier had somehow magically softened to a deep, midnight blue. Gorgeous, delicate saris in gold-flecked yellow and red hung as curtains over the open windows, blowing lightly in the gentle breeze. Scattered around the floor were huge pillows, also covered in the sari fabric, and soft sconces giving a candlelike glow to the room. An intricate gold filigree had been stenciled around the top of all the walls, and from the center of the ceiling hung a huge, wrought-iron chandelier with candles instead of lightbulbs.

Whoa, Sydney thought. *Francie either spent all of her babysitting money from the summer for that, or she has the* best *garage-sale luck in the world.*

Sydney walked to the center of the room, looking around in complete awe. *I thought* I *was busy this week,* she thought. How had Francie managed to accomplish all this in such a short time? Usually, Sydney knew, her roommate was amazing on the planning front but a little hazy on follow-through.

Sydney was so distracted by the room that it took her a moment to notice the note stuck under the answering machine—which was blinking with what looked like a thousand messages. The machine itself, Sydney noticed happily, had been removed from its normal home on a stack of old phonebooks and placed on a low oak side-table—another excellent garage-sale find, Sydney decided.

Sydney put off checking the messages for a minute and turned to the note. Hopefully, she thought, it wouldn't say something like *Dear Sydney—you were gone so long I had to find a new roommate. Good luck!*

In fact, the note almost brought Sydney to tears—but they were happy ones.

Dear Sydney,

I'm hoping that you'll be able to catch that flight back tonight, because I've been missing you SOOOO much. I've actually been leaving a note every time I go anywhere, hoping you'll be home to read it. I know you've been working really hard with your job and I actually feel like I've been really insensitive about it sometimes. I'm going to try to stop bugging you so much. After all, it wouldn't kill me to hit the books a little bit more when you're gone, anyway.

As you can see, we've finished the room! And do you know how? Right after you left,

Brennan brought his entire pledge class in to help me out. They did most of the major stuff, but Brennan really pitched in more than anyone else. I don't think it's a big secret to let you know—he's kind of got a big crush on you! Seriously, when I told him that your business trip was extended, I thought he was going to cry or something, no kidding.

Anyway, don't worry about final registration. You left your book with all the courses you wanted underlined, so I went ahead and got it done for you. I even paid your $75 fee—but I'm sure with all the overtime you worked last week, you're not going to have any trouble getting me back on that one!

Anyway, sweetie, I have a three-hour lab tonight, but I'm hoping you'll be home when I come back! We can get lattes or something, okay?

And I especially hope that you love the room as much as I do—
Love,
Francie

P.S. Call Brennan! He calls every day to ask when you're coming home!!!
Sydney put the note down, not believing how

cool—and un-mad—Francie was being about the whole situation. She'd been dreading having to have another painful heart-to-heart about how much she was working and how hard it was on Francie. Now it looked like Francie had somehow come to terms with the whole situation.

Francie's okay with my working all the time. . . . Noah's not being weird anymore, Sydney thought, taking a seat on one of the new sari-covered cushions. *This is almost as much of an Alice-in-Wonderland world as what just happened with SD-6!*

There was still one thing to take care of, though, obviously, and Sydney wanted to get it out of the way as quickly as possible—she'd gone through too much this past week to stomach any awkward meetings or surprise visits. *If Brennan Daniels is thinking we're going to start something up, I've got to let him down,* Sydney thought. *Gently.*

Brennan's phone number at the frat house was written on a Post-it conveniently stuck to the wall, along with a bunch of other numbers from guys Sydney hadn't ever heard of. *Maybe Francie went ahead and had that party without me already,* Sydney thought with amusement. *I can't imagine living in this awesome pad without needing to throw a few a week.*

The frat's phone kept ringing over and over without any machine picking up. The boys were probably at dinner, Sydney realized. After the fifteenth ring, Sydney was just about to place the receiver on the hook and give up when the phone was answered by a sleepy-sounding frat member.

"Sigma Chi," the young man slurred.

"Yes," Sydney said, hoping that the guy was better about leaving messages than he was at running to get the phone. "I was hoping to speak to Brennan Daniels?"

The phone was suddenly dropped on some hard object—probably the massive kitchen counter Sydney had observed at the party a week ago—without comment. Sydney heard the guy shouting, "Dude! Daniels! Some girl for you!"

Sydney looked around the room and swallowed. There was no doubt she was doing the right thing. But knowing how he had helped Francie did make her feel pretty guilty.

The phone was suddenly jerked up. "Hello?" Brennan said, sounding as hale and chipper as someone standing on the deck of his personal yacht.

"Brennan," Sydney said. "Hi—it's Sydney. Sydney Bristow? I'm just returning your messages." Despite herself, Sydney winced. *God, Syd,* she thought. *Way to rub it in.*

Brennan's voice immediately amped up a notch on the chipper scale. "Sydney! Wow!" He laughed.

"Francie and I thought you were *never* going to come back."

"Well, I'm here," Sydney said. "And I just wanted to call and say thanks for all your help on the room—that was really nice of you. It's beautiful. I don't know how I'm going to ever thank you."

Brennan answered quickly and confidently. "Well, how about letting me bring over a bottle of wine tonight?" he said. "We could drink it with Francie, then maybe go out."

"Francie's not here," Sydney said, then, worried about giving the wrong impression, added, "Um . . . maybe we can all do something tomorrow?"

Oh, you big coward! Sydney chided herself. *You just escaped from two K-Directorate moles who were trying to frame you and get your own boss to put you in jail, and you're afraid of telling a guy who likes you that you don't like him back.*

As if he could read her mind, Brennan persisted, clearly not interested in letting her wriggle out of anything. "Oh, c'mon," he said. "I've got this beautiful bottle of pinot grigio that's been chilling in the fridge, just waiting for you to come home."

Well, I've got to talk to him sometime, Sydney thought. *And Francie's going to be back pretty soon, anyway.*

"Okay," Sydney finally said. "Come over. But you have to give me at least half an hour to take a shower!"

Brennan laughed. "I'm not even going to touch that one," he said. "See you soon."

"See ya," Sydney said.

Twenty minutes later, she was showered, her hair pulled back neatly in a ponytail, and happily dressed in her most comfortable pair of jeans and favorite ratty T-shirt. *Francie would not approve,* Sydney thought. *But she has no idea what kind of week I've been having.*

When the knock came at the door, Sydney reminded herself to keep it short and sweet. *Don't mess it up with a lot of confusing talk like you did with Burke,* she said, thinking of the previous year's boyfriend, who'd fallen by the wayside after a bunch of miscommunications and misunderstandings. *Just tell him there's someone else in your life, and that, even though you really like him, you're not going to be able to be more than friends.*

Over the past year, Sydney had had to learn a lot about guys in general, after all. She still wasn't used to guys hitting on her, or even noticing her at all. *It's natural that you feel awkward,* Sydney told herself, trying to bump up her confidence. *But you still have to do it—if he's been hanging around while you've been away, he's going to want to hang around even more when you're here.*

It wasn't even that Sydney didn't like Brennan, she realized. But looking back on it, she was pretty sure that she'd only been flirting with him because she'd felt so unsure about Noah's feelings for her. It felt shallow to admit it, but it was true: now that she knew Noah felt strongly enough about her to risk everything, she didn't feel anything but a sort of neutral friendliness toward Brennan.

So when Sydney opened the door, Brennan, promised bottle of white wine in hand, looked so eager she could hardly bear to think about how she would let him down.

"Hey," she said, stepping back. Brennan immediately lunged for her cheek, but Sydney turned quickly so that his lips just grazed the place where Noah's had been a scant time ago. "Um, come in and sit down."

Brennan stood awkwardly midlunge for a second, then recovered with a sheepish smile. "Do you have a corkscrew first?" he asked, holding the bottle aloft. "I want to let this breathe."

Sydney closed the door to the hallway and turned around, steeling herself. *Remember, Sydney. Short and sweet. Don't drag it out so the poor guy doesn't know which end is up.*

"Actually, I'd rather just talk without the wine, if that's okay with you," Sydney said, making an effort not to sound bitchy or irritated—even though the fatigue of the day was finally and suddenly getting to her.

Something funny flashed across Brennan's eyes, but he recovered quickly and smiled again, taking a seat on the edge of Francie's bed. Sydney noticed that his dimples, somehow, seemed less alluring this time.

"That doesn't sound good," Brennan tried to joke. "I hope nothing bad happened while you were away."

Sydney took a seat across from him, on another set of pillows that had been placed strategically near the windows, which had a great view of the quad. "No, it's not the trip," she said. "Actually, I wanted to talk about that conversation we had last week—at the party."

Brennan's smile began to look strained. He unclasped his hands, then clasped them again. "Listen, I don't think it's a big mystery that I'm interested in you," Brennan laughed. "But if things are moving too fast for you, I'm fine with slowing them down." He stood and walked over to where Sydney was sitting, putting his hand out for her to shake. "Hell, Sydney, I'd be glad to be just friends."

Sydney laughed and took his hand, incredibly

relieved that it was all going to go pretty easily. "You're being really nice about this," she said, letting Brennan pull her up to a standing position.

"Oh, Sydney," Brennan said, pulling her in for a hug. "You have no idea."

Sydney placed her arms around Brennan's back and gave him a friendly pat. After a few seconds, she tried to withdraw, but Brennan seemed intent on squeezing more. She decided she'd give him a few more seconds—the poor guy.

After all, maybe he's feeling more than he wants to show, Sydney thought. *I know he tries to be so upbeat about everything, but crushes can hit you hard. I mean, look at what happened when I first met Noah.*

But Sydney couldn't hide the fact that Brennan's squeezing was becoming uncomfortable—and making her ribs, still sore from the guards' pushing against them in the car, ache all over again.

"Okay," she said, trying to draw back slightly.

But Brennan only pulled her closer. "Oh, Syd," he whispered. "You have no idea how long we've been waiting for this. Me . . . and Lucy."

The hair on the back of Sydney's neck stood up.

But it was too late. Before she knew it, Brennan had her by the hair, and she heard the click of the blade—it was held against her neck, its metal glinting in the light of Francie's sconces.

"It was you, wasn't it?" Sydney asked, desperately trying to gain some purchase to be able to fling Brennan off of her without tossing them both out the window. "It had nothing to do with Mirofsky—you were the partner!"

"You bet your ass I was," Brennan said, letting the knife dig in slightly to the skin of Sydney's neck. She winced, though out of fear rather than any real pain. "I was more than the partner, to tell you the truth. This was all my idea."

Sydney could feel his grip relax slightly as he warmed to his monologue. She wanted to encourage him to say more—to relax enough that she could get that knife away from him. "Why? Why *was* this your idea?" she asked, keeping her voice down so that Brennan didn't think she was on the verge of shouting for help. "Why me, of all people?"

This was the wrong tack—Brennan only tightened his grip angrily. His lips came very close to Sydney's ear as he held the knife tight against her throat. "You killed the wrong person," Brennan said through his teeth.

Sydney knew whatever change she was waiting for might not come—she had to take her chances now or risk ruining Francie's beautiful room with a lot of ugly blood. "Well, I'm about to kill another one," she said, spinning suddenly against the wall and grabbing the knife. She broke free of Brennan's chokehold on her and jabbed him with two sharp kicks to the torso. The knife skittered away across the floor.

"You're scum," Brennan gasped. "Criminal."

Sydney stopped midpunch—she'd been about to finish him off with her right cross. "I'm CIA," she said, breathing heavily from the exertion. "*You're* the one working for K-Directorate."

And Brennan, astonishingly, began to laugh. "That's the biggest joke I've heard in my life." He made a lunge for the knife.

But Sydney had already grabbed the wine bottle, still cold from Sigma Chi's refrigerator. "You won't be laughing when you meet my boss," she said, bringing the bottle down on his head with all her strength.

As Brennan lay whimpering on the floor, Sydney pocketed the knife and looked around for Francie's suitcase. If she knew her friend, it was still shoved, half unpacked, under her bed. *I don't think Sigma Chi got far enough to start unpacking all of Francie's clothes,* she thought, scrambling under the bed for the suitcase, which, thank God, seemed to be in evidence.

That Child*Leash system was about to come in handy.

CIA

FROM THE DESK OF JACK BRISTOW

I AM VERY SADDENED TO REPORT THAT WE HAVE LOST TWO VALU-
ABLE AGENTS THIS WEEK: ANYA MIROFSKY AND DANIEL BRENNAN.

AS YOU KNOW, ANYA MIROFSKY WAS WORKING CLOSELY WITH OUR
TEAM IN A HIGH-LEVEL SURVEILLANCE AND INFILTRATION OF ARVIN
SLOANE OF SD-6. FROM THE INFORMATION WE HAVE SO FAR, WE'VE
GLEANED THAT DURING A STANDOFF, SOMETHING WENT WRONG. WE
ARE STILL INVESTIGATING THE EXACT CIRCUMSTANCES, BUT WE DO
KNOW THAT ANYA LOST HER LIFE IN A GUN BATTLE.

I AM ALSO SADDENED TO REPORT THE DEATH OF VALUABLE TEAM
MEMBER DANIEL BRENNAN. AS WE ALL KNOW, DANIEL HAD A DIFFICULT
TIME ADJUSTING AFTER THE DEATH OF HIS PARTNER, PAUL RZHEVSKY,
DURING THE INFILTRATION OF SD-2 LAST SPRING. IT SEEMS VERY POSSI-
BLE THAT HE COULD NO LONGER HANDLE HIS GRIEF. I AM VERY SORRY TO
REPORT THAT, SOMETIME THIS WEEKEND, HE TOOK HIS OWN LIFE.

COUNSELORS ARE AVAILABLE FOR ANY EMPLOYEES WHO FEEL THEY
NEED TO TALK TO SOMEONE.

I still can't believe I was able to maintain a straight face when Sydney hauled in "Brennan Daniels" for me to "discipline."

I'm not surprised that he turned out to be behind this whole mess, now that I think about it. In fact, I'd like to slap myself for not seeing something like this coming sooner. His tips were useless—always items that seemed as if they'd be useful to me, but had either lost their currency or were slightly off. Usually just the mark of the inexperienced tipster, so I can't fault myself too much for not thinking anything of it.

Still, I'm highly displeased with the way he got to Lucy. Compromising my new tech . . . assassinating a valuable new employee . . . and almost causing me to get rid of Sydney.

And all to get a higher price from K-Directorate. As if SD-6 couldn't match K-Directorate dollar for dollar.

And, actually, that's the most amusing part of this entire situation. Because, even though this entire operation was more **chaotic** than I usually like for my smaller missions, we were in no danger of losing any information on the scalar pulse gun to K-Directorate, for the simple reason that we were never looking for any information on a scalar pulse gun.

Radikovitch was a hack, everyone knows that. The chances of finding anything technologically useful to us now in that madman's old files were about the same as the chances of our finding a physicist working at a Starbucks.

Except for the fact that the old coot was pretty interested in **Rambaldi.**

I've already found a hint of some leads in one of his letters to his niece. I hope to find more soon.

Let's hope K-Directorate is happy with whatever they got out of it. But if they think they're looking for leads for the pulse gun, then they didn't get much.

Speaking of which, I cannot even express how relieved I was that Sydney turned out to be clean. I'm not sure I would have been surprised—she's such a smart, able, talented girl. She would be the first to be pulled away by a more lucrative opportunity.

After all, she may be her father's daughter—but she's also her mother's.

But I had run the numbers and had my heart-to-heart with myself. There's no other way to put it—she was definitely marked for **deletion.**

I can't say I'm glad that Noah disregarded my orders, but I suppose that's what love will do to you. I'm going to have to keep an even closer eye on their relationship now than I already have been.

Knowing that Sydney's still entirely on board also solves another one of my problems. Because if Sydney had had an "accident," Jack Bristow would have been the wild card. I'm still not sure how we would have dealt with that—and that's what kept me from doing anything too extreme to Sydney the minute that tape of the Berlin files surfaced.

And I'm a patient, generous man. You know, sending a quivering Daniel Brennan home, and then later, standing over him in his apartment as he slept, for a moment, I even considered keeping him on.

But he hadn't made himself useful.

And he'd obviously caused a lot of problems.

Speaking of which, our problems with K-Directorate will continue. At least the CIA seems to be losing its juice. It seems that they're always two steps behind. Perhaps there's just no reason to worry about that dinosaur of an organization anymore.

Not until they get some agents that SD-6 can't defeat easily, that is.

You know, it occurs to me that Sydney Bristow really had a guardian angel in this case. She was lucky, quite lucky. She's got a lot of people watching over her. A lot of people with her best interests at heart.

More than most people in this business.

Okay, this was **scary**. Really scary. My cocoon at school was safe. Protected from all the weirdness that goes on at SD-6.

And now it's been horribly, irrevocably violated.

At least I was able to defeat the bad guy. But the fact that Brennan crept—no, slithered—into my world makes me really nervous. There's no way I'm letting anything like this occur again. Letting my guard down—no way. Not going to happen.

My time at UCLA with Francie is the one **sacred** thing I have in my life. Here, I don't have to worry about saving the world. Here, my worries are about frat boys and English exams and keeping Francie's clothes off my bed. That's the way it should be.

And Noah and SD-6 . . . well, that's the way it should be too. They both keep me on my toes. They're helping me to be strong. Powerful. And to give me a greater purpose than I could ever have imagined. I am an agent for the United States of America. Home of the free and the brave—home to those who fight for it, every step of the way.

The **entire world** is at my feet.

Time to start walking.